"You

friend...

Oh, Lord, he smelled wonderful. Silvey unabashedly buried her nose in the V opening of his shirt.

"That depends." Dan's lips feathered over her temple.

"Depends on what?"

"On how much you want it."

His nearness was fogging up her mind. "Oh, I want it." She sighed.

With a soft chuckle, Dan brought his mouth to hers.

When he finally pulled away and looked down at her, his deep blue eyes were filled with amusement. "I'd say, on the friendliness factor, that kiss rates ten."

Dear Reader,

Fifteen years ago I took a class in which several people were interested in writing contemporary romance novels. The most discussed books were from Harlequin Romance and Presents. I had never heard of these books, so I borrowed some—and fell instantly in love. They were wonderful; the heroes always strong, the heroines always winners, the stories full of emotional impact and exotic locales. I read hundreds of them—bought new ones by the dozen and borrowed old ones from friends and from the library. Thank goodness Harlequin had, by then, been publishing Romance for twenty-five years. There were plenty of books to feed my newfound hunger!

Now 1997 marks the tenth anniversary of my first sale to Harlequin, and A *Double Wedding* is my tenth Harlequin Romance title. I hope you'll agree that in this fortieth year of Harlequin Romance, we're not getting older, we're getting better!

Happy reading

Patricia Knoll

A Double Wedding
Patricia Knoll

Harlequin Books

TORONTO • NEW YORK • LONDON
AMSTERDAM • PARIS • SYDNEY • HAMBURG
STOCKHOLM • ATHENS • TOKYO • MILAN
MADRID • WARSAW • BUDAPEST • AUCKLAND

This book is dedicated to Karla Knoll Laird because
she's the next best thing to a sister.

ISBN 0-373-03462-8

A DOUBLE WEDDING

First North American Publication 1997.

Copyright © 1997 by Patricia Knoll.

CHAPTER ONE

CAPRICIOUS desert winds tossed sprinkles of rain and handfuls of dirt at the big plate-glass windows of The Yogurt Gallery. Fine dust sifted in around the edges of the door.

Dismayed, Silvanna Carlton gazed at the expanse of glass she had polished to perfection that morning, then down to the black-and-white tile floor she had mopped only moments ago.

Muttering disparaging comments about Arizona's erratic summer weather, she dipped her string mop back into the sudsy, pine-scented water and picked her way circumspectly to the door. With gentle swings of her slim hips, she dodged the little white tables and wrought-iron chairs. She used broad swipes of the mop to swab the area where the dust had already turned to mud. Grimly, she vowed to get new insulation on the doorframe as soon as the final papers were signed and the shop belonged to her.

The thought sent satisfied joy surging through her. Her shop. Her floor, windows, equipment. Her own business, at last.

The smile she flashed around the room changed her oval face from pretty to striking, and brought sparkling lights to her brown eyes. Catching sight of herself in the window, she blew her froth of golden brown bangs out of her face and laughed

5

out loud as she realized that her expression could only be described as smug.

Mop in hand, she stepped back to the dry part of the floor to survey her work. Satisfaction and happiness tingled through her in equal measure. She felt so restless and excited that she could have done a handstand and a backflip off one of the little tables. Instead, she pirouetted in an impromptu dance, holding on to the mop handle as if it was her partner. Exuberantly, she swung around like Ginger Rogers in one of the old musicals she loved.

For a moment, she forgot that her feet ached all the way up to her shoulders. She remembered only that three years after the end of her career as a circus acrobat, and many interim jobs that she'd found unsatisfactory, she had found one she loved—managing this shop. She had wanted a settled and stable life, and now she was going to have it.

The Yogurt Gallery was perfect for her. Besides meeting interesting people as she worked behind the counter, she had contact with local artisans who placed all types of artwork, from stained glass to oil paintings, for the shop to sell on consignment. Her outgoing personality made her popular with the customers and her artistic soul was drawn to the craftsmen and their work.

The shop's location attracted a steady stream of patrons thanks to its location in a minimall. People came in for a cold snack and for some relief from Tucson's searing summer heat. With all those factors working for her, she just knew she could make a go of the shop on her own.

She laughed, and her air castles dissipated like wisps of smoke before the reality that she had to buy the shop first, but at least it was possible now. Thanks to Grandma, who had come up with the money that very day, bless her!

Mop in hand, Silvey was turning toward the back room when someone tapped on the window.

A man stood peering in, his hands bracketing his eyes. She couldn't get a clear view of his face, but glimpsed a flash of white shirt and dark slacks.

Startled, she shouted, "We're closed!"

The man's hands dropped to cup his mouth. "Open up. I need...." Whatever he said was drowned out by another glass-rattling gust of wind.

Silvey shook her head firmly. "Sorry, we're closed." She tiptoed across the damp floor to shut the miniblinds.

The man must have thought she was going to open the door because he stepped back expectantly, looking down at the knob. When she reached for the cord to close the blinds, he yelled, "Hey, wait," and lunged forward.

Silvey got a glimpse of a strongly defined face and angry eyes behind dark-rimmed glasses before she let the miniblinds fall down, twisted the wand, and stepped away from the door.

It was almost eleven o'clock at night, for goodness' sake, and the shop's hours were clearly posted by the door.

She stood still for a moment, wondering if the stranger had gone, reluctant to peek out. "I'll be darned if I'm going to be a prisoner in my own shop," she muttered. She pulled back a corner of the blind and saw him disappearing down the sidewalk. Relieved, she rinsed the mop and bucket and put them away in the back room, then took window cleaner and a soft cloth to give the gleaming glass and stainless steel cases one more shine.

Ordinarily, she didn't close up, depending on the part-time high school and college-age employees to do that for her. But today she had worked straight through from opening time until closing because some of her employees were on vacation, and the others couldn't cover until tomorrow.

Silvey spread the cloth over the edge of the sink and gripped the cool stainless steel. She stiffened her arms until they quivered and dropped her head forward, attempting to ease the strain between her shoulders. Finally, she straightened, rubbed her neck, and yawned.

The last few months had been the most hectic of her life. Walter, the owner, had been sick, leaving most of the responsibility for running the business to her.

She had thought it would be easy to buy her own business. Now she shook her head at her naiveté.

It hadn't helped that her only previous long-term job had been as an acrobat in a circus. As far as she was concerned, it was a perfectly respectable job, but she admitted it wasn't known for its stability. After all, she'd lost that job when the circus went bankrupt.

Since leaving the circus three years ago she had held a string of jobs and that history had also worked against her when she had tried to get a loan.

When the loan officer had called earlier and broken the news that the bank considered her a poor risk, she had been heartsick and called her grandmother for sympathy. Grandma phoned back two hours later to say the money was being deposited into their joint account that very day.

Silvey had been stunned, bubbling with questions, which had to go unanswered because she had a shopful of customers. She was eager to get home and find out where Grandma had come across such a windfall.

Because there was so much to talk over, she hoped her grandmother didn't have a houseful of late-staying guests. Grandma's string of eccentric friends would be in the way tonight. Although, now that she thought about it, those friends hadn't been around much lately.

Silvey frowned as she double-checked the door locks and flipped off the lights. Grandma had been acting odd lately—well, odd for someone who was always a bit off the wall. She had been quiet, almost dreamy, not her usual vocal self, spouting about the injustices being done to the elderly, or to laboratory animals, or about her new cause: preserving Arizona Indian burial grounds and artifacts.

Anxious to get home, Silvey picked up the zippered bag for the bank's night deposit slot, pulled her purse strap up over her shoulder, set the alarm, and went out the back door. Late-night heat radiated upward from the asphalt that had absorbed it all day and was now releasing it. For the moment, the wind had settled down.

After locking the door behind her, she turned to leave the alley. The moon was hidden by clouds and the light at the end of the alley was burned out. She had mentioned it to the shopping center's owners, fearing for her teenage employees who worked late, but it had yet to be fixed.

Tomorrow, she would complain again, long and loud. She stepped up her pace, intending to make her deposit quickly and hop into her car. Thank goodness she had recently been able to afford a new, dependable one. The sporty Mazda Rx 7 might have been extravagant, but she'd been offered a great deal on it from an old boyfriend who sold what he said were mint-condition, preowned cars.

Of course, if she hadn't bought the car, she might not have needed such a large loan to buy the shop. She shrugged her tired shoulders and trudged down the alley.

The breeze picked up again, scattering trash and rattling fronds on a stand of palm trees. They reached spiky fingers into the night sky as if to puncture the fat clouds scudding overhead, hiding, then revealing, the moon.

Silvey lifted her head and sniffed the air. The rain-freshened wind picked up again, spreading the sharp, sweet smell of wet mesquite and pungent creosote.

A dull, metallic thud sounded behind her and she glanced back over her shoulder. Probably some of the cats that patrolled the trash Dumpsters. As she watched, a shadow wavered.

Disturbed, Silvey whipped around and walked faster, moving just short of a run through the dark alley, heading for the light. "Maybe it's nothing," she muttered. "But...oof!"

Silvey bounced off a solid body and staggered backward, the breath punched from her lungs. Even as she heard the other person grunt in surprise, she stumbled against a wall.

Dazed, she tilted her head back to see a man standing over her. His face was harsh in the yellow glow of the halogen parking lot lights. Dark-rimmed glasses made it hard for her to see his eyes. His hand was reaching out to touch her shoulder.

In that instant, she recognized him as the man who had been watching her through the shop window. She jerked back, scrambling along the wall to get away.

"I won't hurt you," he insisted. "Was someone chasing you?"

She blinked, taken by surprise once again. "No...no...." She hated to admit it since she now seemed to be faced with a man who was more daunting than anything she could have met in that alley. "I'm fine. I guess I just got spooked," she said with a defensive upthrust of her chin. "Especially after seeing you at the front door of my shop earlier, Mr....?"

"My name's Dan."

She nodded and gripped the strap of her shoulder bag. The zippered bank envelope shifted under her arm. The gesture reminded her that she had yet to make her bank deposit.

Nervously, she clutched it and edged away, eyeing him cautiously. There was money in that pouch. She breathed a silent, relieved breath when he stepped back to give her some space. "Well, thank you for your help, Mr., uh, Dan. Good night."

"Wait, Miss Carlton. I need to talk to you."

He knew her name! That stopped her, swinging her around in alarm. "Exactly what is it you want?'' They were directly under one of the lights now and she stared up into his face. She tried for the freezing look her grandmother could use to such effect.

"Just to talk to you."

Silvey didn't budge. "What do you need to talk to me about?"

"It's a personal matter. I tried to get you to listen earlier, but you wouldn't open the door."

"One of my brighter moves," she murmured uncertainly. "I don't even know you."

"That's easily solved."

She drew her bottom lip under her teeth, then turned away with a shake of her head. "Go away. Come back during business hours. *Daylight* business hours. I'm tired and I'm going home. And don't follow me!" She hurried off, finally reaching the dubious comfort and safety of the parking lot. Relieved, she rushed toward the bank.

"Please, Miss Carlton. I'm not going to hurt you." He swung around in front of her and held his hands up as if to prove it.

At least she could see him better now. His features appeared hard under the yellow lights, all bones and angles. His hair was thick, and cut short. He was dressed in dark slacks and a light shirt with its long sleeves rolled up.

"If I'd wanted to try something, I would have done it in the alley," he said pointedly, removing his glasses and frowning at her. "This won't take much of your time and I'm sure we can resolve things to our mutual satisfaction."

"Resolve what things?"

He slipped his glasses on. His eyes seemed to pierce her through the lenses. "You'll find out sooner if you cooperate." As if her agreement was a foregone conclusion, he moved aside. "I'll wait while you make your bank deposit."

Unnerved by the whole incident in the alley, the touch of his hand, his persistence, and straightforward watchfulness, Silvey whipped the pouch behind her back. His brows arched at her defensiveness.

He lifted his hands slowly away from his sides and did a slow turn to show her he carried no weapon. When he spoke, his voice was low, humoring her. "I'm not after your money. In fact, it's the other way around, isn't it?"

"What?" She pulled back, puzzled.

"I mean just what I said."

"You haven't *said* anything."

He only smiled again, his mouth as controlled as the rest of him.

Curiosity warred with caution. Who was this guy and what did he want? There was only one way to find out. Caution went down to defeat, but Silvey was determined to at least give the appearance of being in control of the situation. "All right," she finally said in a crisp tone.

She headed toward the bank and he walked several feet away from her, then waited at the edge of the sidewalk while she unlocked the night deposit slot and slipped the bag inside. Relieved to be rid of it, she looked back to him.

"I want to have this talk in a public place." She pointed to a twenty-four-hour restaurant across the parking lot.

"Whatever you say."

Silvey started off at a fast clip. Her spirits rose as they drew near the brightly lit building where she often ate when Grandma's friends had cleaned out the refrigerator or when her own lack of culinary skill got the better of her.

Dan held the door for her and she skirted him. He tilted his head in sardonic acknowledgment of her evasive tactic, but she ignored him, welcoming the lights and the quiet sounds of cutlery and dishes being washed. The place smelled of strong coffee and the same pine cleaner she used on her own shop floors. It was almost deserted with only a few late-night stragglers occupying scattered booths. A waitress came forward with menus.

"Hi, Silvey. Working late tonight, hmm?"

"No choice, Patsy, when the part-timers are on vacation." Silvey's mood lightened to amusement when the waitress's interest skipped over her and landed on Dan.

The voltage of Patsy's smile went up several notches. "Welcome. Just sit anywhere. I'll be with you in a minute."

Silvey looked at Dan—and to discover what the waitress found so attractive in him. With the brighter lights smoothing out the angles in his face, he was almost handsome. His features were even, not harsh. Sandy brown hair was combed straight back from his deeply tanned face. Sky-blue eyes met her surprised brown ones and amusement flickered momentarily. She couldn't begin to guess his age. He appeared to be somewhere around thirty, but his eyes seemed older—watchful.

They started toward a booth at the back of the homey restaurant which was decorated with chintz curtains and hanging plants. The two of them slid into opposite sides of a red vinyl booth.

Dan flipped open the menu. "What will you have?"

"Just coffee, please." Silvey watched him for a long minute as she experienced the same uneasy sensations she'd known in the parking lot.

He ordered coffee for both of them and Silvey said, "Now, why don't you get to the point and tell me what you want?"

He met her direct gaze with one of his own. His eyes darkened to the hue of midnight as they searched her small, piquant features, lined with cautious suspicion. Finally, he nodded. "All right." From his shirt pocket, he drew a small notebook. "Just let me confirm a few facts to make sure I have the right woman."

She straightened away from the cool vinyl seat. "Right woman?"

"You are Silvanna Lee Carlton, aged twenty-three?"

"Well, yes, but...."

"Your parents, Richard and Elaine Carlton currently live in Venezuela where they work as geologists for Marathon Oil company?"

Silvey's hands gripped the edge of the table. "How do you know about my parents?"

He plowed ahead. "You live with your grandmother, Leila Parkins Carlton, also known as Leila the Wonder Woman, a former circus acrobat, with whom you performed for several years, and with whom you now have a joint bank account?"

Silvey's brown eyes grew enormous with surprise. "Well, certainly she used that name when we were in the circus...but what business is it of yours about our bank account?" She half rose from her seat. "What's this all about? Who are you?"

A lock of hair had fallen over his forehead, but it did nothing to soften his features. His face was inscrutable as he watched the confusion that drew her brows together and dropped the corners of her mouth into a pout. His look flicked from her lips and narrowed on her puzzled eyes.

"My last name is Wisdom, and I want to know what it will cost me to keep you and your grandmother away from my father."

"Your father? Who on earth is your father?"

"Lawrence Wisdom, as if you didn't know."

"Well, I certainly don't know. I've never heard of him. Or you. And I never want to hear *from* you again. You are a crazy man. I should have trusted my first instinct and refused to talk to you." She started to rise.

Dan sat forward, pinning her with the strength of his will. His fingers gripped the edge of the table until the tips whitened. When he spoke, he made sure only his voice touched her, low and scathing. "Sit down, Miss Carlton, and listen to what I have to say."

She stared at him, engaged in an inner battle. Part of her wanted to sweep out on a tide of righteous indignation. A larger part wanted to defend her grandmother's reputation as well as her own.

"I'm listening," she said.

The waitress bustled up with her pot of steaming coffee. When she started to speak, Dan gave her an impatient glance. Startled, she poured the coffee and hurried away.

Silvey knew that Patsy must have felt the tension between them. It was as thick as ozone during a summer lightening storm.

With her gone, and sure of Silvey's compliance, the set of Dan's shoulders eased and he inclined his head. "I've been out of town for several weeks—just got back today. And found out about Leila Carlton's relationship with my father."

Silvey started to protest but he held up a hand. "I came to talk to you because I'm a reasonable man. I'm willing to give her whatever amount of money she wants if she'll leave him alone—and, of course, I'll give you an equal amount." His eyes flicked over her. "Within reason, of course."

Silvey stared at him, her eyes wide. She opened her mouth to speak, but no words came. She'd never been offered money like this from a total stranger—or anyone else for that matter. It was so insulting it was laughable. She swallowed and tried again.

"None of this makes sense. Why don't we start from the beginning, Mr. Wisdom? There's obviously been some kind of mistake here. Your father is involved with some woman...."

"Leila Parkins Carlton."

"That's impossible," she scoffed. "I would know if Grandma had started seeing a man."

"Oh, they only met recently." Dan steepled his hands on the tabletop. "They've been corresponding for a number of weeks." His glance came up and focused. "She seems to have learned only lately of his last divorce."

"His last...?" She paused, then gasped, making the connection. "Lawrence Wisdom, the *actor*?" Her voice shot up two octaves. "That... that...lecher?"

CHAPTER TWO

DAN jerked forward, ready for battle. White lines appeared around his mouth and nose, but before he could speak, she went on.

"You really are nuts if you think I'll believe Grandma is involved with that old . . . tomcat."

Silvey was flabbergasted. Lawrence Wisdom had been a famous swashbuckling movie actor in the forties and fifties. The roles he chose now were more staid and mature, but he hadn't slowed down yet in his lovelife. He had made a much-publicized move to Tucson the year before, saying he wanted to leave the Hollywood life-style behind. About time, too, Silvey thought, since he was well into his seventies.

Watching her expression, the narrow lines of Dan's face coalesced into a mask of contempt. "You'd better watch what phraseology you use, Miss Carlton. There are words for you and your grandmother, too, such as gold digger and opportunist."

"Gold digger?" Color washed out of her face, then rushed back in a crimson flood. She arched over the table and stabbed a finger at his chest. "I've got news for you, mister. The Carltons aren't wealthy but we do just fine, thank you, and we're not interested in anybody else's money."

"I've heard that before."

"Well, this time, believe it, because it's true!"

As they argued, he, too, had risen and they were leaning toward each other. Mere inches separated them. Silvey could see the pupils in his eyes contract to pinpoints.

She knew she was very close to losing control, but she let the anger take her, anyway. "Just who do you think you are? What gives you the right to make these accusations against someone you don't even know?"

Dan straightened slowly, sat back down, and crossed his arms over his chest. He clasped his biceps and looked more formidable than ever. "I do what I have to in order to protect my father."

"From me and my seventy-two-year-old, white-haired *grandma*?" Silvey splayed a hand over her chest, then shook her head and continued. "You've worked very hard to protect your father, and that's admirable. I would certainly do the same." At the swift hardening of his features, she realized she was taking the wrong approach and hurried to add, "The problem is, you've got the wrong people."

"I have proof." From his pocket, he drew a folded piece of paper. With exact gestures, he opened and smoothed it, then handed it over.

Silvey cast him a suspicious glance, but accepted it. It was a photostatic copy of a typed letter. Her gaze flew down to find the identical twin of her grandmother's signature at the bottom. Uneasily, she studied it, then her eyes rose to Dan Wisdom's expectant face. She returned to the letter.

It gushed, so full of syrupy phrasing she was amazed the paper didn't stick to her fingers. The writer told Lawrence Wisdom how she had admired him through the years, commiserated with him over the breakup of his latest marriage, and asked if they could meet. The writer said she worked with a group concerned with a number of environmental and social issues, and asked if he would be interested in joining. Silvey frowned, studying the signature that looked more convincing the longer she gazed at it, and began to have doubts about her adamant denials.

Grandma *had* been acting strange lately. She had gone to a trendy hairdresser who cut the long hair she had worn for years in a neat bun. It was now short and sleek. Her closet was filling up with new, chic clothing to go with the stylish cut. Though she had always been in good shape—as a circus acrobat a gain of only a few pounds could make the difference between a successful routine and a bomb— Leila had taken up race walking.

And, strangest of all, she had begun suggesting Silvey call her by her first name!

Silvey glanced at Dan, then once again at the letter. Impossible! Someone must have used Leila's name and forged her signature; she couldn't possibly have written that letter herself. She was a senior citizen, for goodness' sake! She simply didn't chase men, especially men with the type of unsavory reputation Lawrence Wisdom had. And yet . . . that signature looked so real.

Her face composed, Silvey folded the letter and handed it back.

Dan returned it to his pocket, propped his elbows on the table, and spread his hands wide as if her agreement was a foregone conclusion. "Well, was I right?"

His certainty only fueled hers. "Of course not. My grandmother would never have written anything like that in a million years."

"You're an obstinate woman, Miss Carlton," he said on a sigh. He glanced away, dropped his hands, and began drumming his fingers on the table. "But there's no point in denying that your grandmother wrote that letter."

"Why would she write instead of call? They live in the same city."

"He's a celebrity," her adversary noted reasonably, removing the letter once again and holding it between his fingers. "His number's not listed. Also, he was in California for several weeks, wrapping up a movie."

"And mopping up his last messy divorce," Silvey supplied sourly.

Dan hissed an exasperated breath. "Which cost him a great deal of money. Is that what your grandmother wants, too, a nice, fat, divorce settlement?"

Silvey was so furious she could barely speak. "Absolutely not!"

Dan shoved back the coffee cup he had been fidgeting with. His gaze seared into hers. "What about you? What are you interested in? As if I didn't know," he snorted. "How do you explain the sizable deposit to your bank account today?"

Silvey's hot retort died unspoken. How had he known about that? She had no answer because she didn't know where the money had come from. "My finances are none of your business," she bluffed. "How did you find out all this information about us?"

His gaze sharpened as if he sensed he was getting somewhere. "As I said, I was away. My father's housekeeper picked up my mail, checked on my house. When I dropped by Dad's place to get my things, that letter was mixed up with my mail. And when I showed it to him, he confessed everything."

"Confessed, hmm? Was that before or after you used the thumbscrews on him?"

Dan's jaw became as hard as granite. "I'm protecting him." He stood suddenly, reached into his pocket, and withdrew several bills which he threw on the table. "There's only one way to solve this. We'll go ask your grandmother."

He started from the restaurant. With a squeak of protest, Silvey scrambled after him. "Wait a minute. She's probably asleep."

Dan was at the door by this time, but he glanced over his shoulder. "Then we'll simply wake her up."

"Well, of all the..." she sputtered, but found she was talking to the silently closing glass door. Running after him, she gave the door a stiff-armed shove. She reached the parking lot hot on his heels and discovered that he was parked right beside her.

"If the house is dark, you're not to wake her," Silvey insisted. "Older people need their sleep." He ignored her as he unlocked his car.

Surrendering, she threw her hands in the air. "I won't bother to give you directions," she said hotly. "I'm sure you know where it is."

Beneath the yellow glow of the parking lot lights, she saw him nod. "As a matter of fact, I do."

They both climbed into their cars and Silvey led the way, fuming all the while. Lawrence Wisdom might be in hot pursuit by some female, but it wasn't Leila. Grandma would have told her if she'd begun dating someone. She never dated. Silvey's fertile brain couldn't even form a picture of her grandmother going out on a date, and especially not with someone as famous—or infamous—as Lawrence Wisdom.

If her car could have operated on the energy produced by Silvey's furious thoughts, she would have flown home. As it was, she zipped down the nearly empty streets and bit back a curse as she pulled onto her own. The driveway of the home she and her grandmother shared, as well as several of their neighbors' driveways, was being resurfaced. Temporarily, they had to park on the street, already packed with cars.

She managed to find a tight spot to squeeze her little Mazda into. Let Mr. Nosey Wisdom find his own place. She jumped out of her car and discovered that to her further irritation, he solved the problem by double-parking directly across from her house.

Well, fine. Maybe he would get a traffic ticket.

They met on the front walk of the house and she pointed a finger at him. "I don't know where you got this crazy idea, mister, but we're going to straighten it out right now! My grandmother isn't the type to chase anyone, or write the kind of letter you're flashing around." Silvey marched up the walk, flung the door open and plunged inside. "She's a woman of principle!"

Her ringing announcement might have carried more weight if her grandmother hadn't been standing in the middle of the living room kissing a total stranger.

"Grandma!"

"Dad!"

Silvey's gaze shot to the astounded face of the man behind her, then swung back to the couple that had sprung apart as if they'd been halved by a cleaver.

"Silvanna."

"Daniel."

Dan placed his hands on his waist and said, "Well, now that we've established everyone's identities, why don't you run through a couple of quick explanations, Dad?"

Silvey could only stare helplessly while Leila smoothed her fluffed hair, pursed her kiss-swollen lips, and straightened the blue cotton top she wore over her new designer jeans. "I'd like you to meet Lawrence Wisdom."

Silvey finally found her voice as she stared in bewilderment. "I get the impression we should have met some weeks ago."

"Dad, you promised to go slowly this time." Dan ran his hand through his sandy hair in a gesture so harsh he should have plucked out every strand.

The tall, handsome man with the thick mane of white hair, piercing blue eyes, and a trim waist looked so offended that guilt surged through Silvey. She quickly reminded herself that he was a professional actor. Manufactured emotions were his stock in trade.

His answer came out in ringing tones. If he'd been onstage, he could have been heard in the back row of a distant balcony. "Son, I *am* going slowly. My beautiful Leila and I have known each other for an entire month and we aren't even engaged yet.'' He turned to Silvey and swept her a courtly bow. ''Miss Carlton, it's a pleasure to meet you at last.''

Silvey dropped her purse onto an overstuffed chair and sank down beside it with a groan of despair. ''Oh, Grandma.'' Everything she had told Dan Wisdom, every impassioned defense had turned out to be a lie. When she looked at his face, though, he didn't look happy at being proven right. In fact, he looked as sick and frustrated as she felt.

That silly, sappy letter he had shown her really had been written by her scatty grandparent. What could Leila have been thinking when she had begun pursuing a man like this? Silvey looked up at Lawrence's face as he confronted his son. He was still a good-looking devil, appearing years younger than what she knew him to be.

''What are you doing here, anyway, Daniel?''

''Proving to Miss Carlton that the two of you have a thing going,'' he answered. ''Dad, after all you told me earlier, did you think I wouldn't look into it?''

Lawrence Wisdom's brows drew together and he shifted his feet uncomfortably, but he seemed to be without an answer.

Silvey watched as Leila smiled and stepped forward to take Lawrence's arm. ''This is your son? The college professor?''

Silvey looked at him in surprise. College professor?

''Yes, this is Daniel.'' Pride rang in the older man's voice. There was obviously a great deal of affection between the two of them. She could admire that if she let herself. But she wouldn't, she decided, straightening her shoulders.

No matter what Dan might think of Leila, someone had drilled manners into him. He shook the hand Leila offered as his serious gaze searched her face intently. "How do you do?"

"Lawrence speaks so highly of you, my dear. Of your intelligence and dedication to your job. He's quite proud of you."

Dan gave his father a long-suffering look. "Yeah, well, he's quite a specimen, himself."

Leila's hands fluttered to her waist. "Oh, well, yes, he certainly is."

Amazed to see her feisty, outspoken relative at a loss for words, Silvey rose. "Mr. Wisdom," she began, speaking to Dan.

"It's Dr. Wisdom," his proud parent broke in.

"Dr. Wisdom," she corrected. "It appears that perhaps you were right and I was wrong." She gave him a quick look, then glanced away. She didn't know what to make of all this. She wished the two men would leave so she could collect her thoughts.

"So it seems." Dan answered her with another piercing look, then turned to his father. "Dad, we'd better go now. We need to talk, and I think Miss Carlton wants to speak to her grandmother."

"Oh, of course," Lawrence said, and reached for Leila's hands. He drew her forward, and kissed her once again.

Silvey glanced at Dan, who was watching the older couple with a closed expression. Giving her a dismissive look, he stepped to the door, swung it open, and held it, allowing a warm breeze in. Fingers drumming the knob, he waited for his father, who finally parted from Leila, said good-night to Silvey, and stepped outside.

Dan didn't look back or say good-night, and neither did Silvey.

As the men's steps faded down the walk, Silvey rounded on Leila, hands on hips. "Why didn't you tell me about this, Grandma?"

"Leila," she corrected with a saucy grin.

Silvey closed her eyes and prayed for patience as her grandmother walked over to fluff the sofa cushions. Her full lips pulled together as she imagined what kind of activity had crushed them. "All right, Leila. Why didn't you tell me you had met this man?" She recalled the letter. "Chased this man?"

Leila sat down and folded her hands. "Several reasons," she admitted. "I didn't know how you'd react to a man in my life. After all, you were very close to your grandfather."

Silvey nodded, still frowning. "Yes, but I would have understood, or tried to. Besides, it's been five years."

"Also, I wanted to see where things would lead...."

"I've got an idea where they're leading," Silvey sputtered, eyeing the sofa.

Leila gave her a quelling look, reminiscent of her usual iron will. "All right, maybe I wanted to keep it to myself for a while."

To savor falling in love again. Silvey didn't need to hear the words to know it was true. There was a softness about Leila that she hadn't noticed before.

"But why Lawrence Wisdom, of all people? He's had a battalion of wives!"

Clearly affronted, Leila drew herself up. "Don't be ridiculous. Those silly young things were merely ego-flattering diversions. Trophy wives. They only wanted alimony from him. I've already told him I have no interest in his money."

Silvey's eyes widened. "But you do! What Dan said is true, isn't it? The money you got for me to buy the shop was from Lawrence, wasn't it?"

"Yes." Leila examined her nails, lacquered in bright fuchsia polish, then she gave Silvey a troubled look. "Lawrence said he had told his son about the wonderful investment he had made today, but the boy stormed out without waiting for an explanation."

And stormed straight over to Silvey's shop. Thoughtfully, she pinched her bottom lip between her thumb and forefinger. No wonder Dan had been upset.

Seeing that Silvey was worried about Lawrence's loan, Leila went on. "To him, it's an investment. You'll pay him back."

"Of course, but . . ."

"No buts about it. It's a straightforward business deal. His attorney will draw up a contract and you and I will hire one to look it over."

It sounded good, but Silvey wasn't sure. How could she accept a loan from Lawrence Wisdom? She didn't even know him.

Leila studied Silvey's frown. "Don't worry, honey. Although you never see it in the tabloids, Lawrence has helped a number of young entrepreneurs get started."

"But did he date their grandmothers?"

"It's business!"

"With a few fringe benefits."

"Yes, a few. For me."

Silvey stared at the soft joy glowing in her grandmother's face. Uncomfortable before it, she stood and mumbled something about needing sleep. She walked slowly to her room.

This was going to take some adjustment—and she wasn't the only one who would have to adjust. Dan Wisdom would, too. Thinking uncomplimentary thoughts about men who threw around words like "gold digger" and "opportunist," she began getting ready for bed.

The next morning, Silvey staggered out of bed and into the shower. Functioning by feel alone, she washed her hair, then let the water pound down on her scalp. Worry about her grandmother's involvement with Lawrence Wisdom and about the rightness of accepting the loan from him had kept her awake.

After she was showered and dressed, she headed to the kitchen where she made toast and coffee, retrieved the newspaper from the front walk, and glanced at the headlines as she ate. With a sigh, she folded the paper and set it aside. Nothing in the national news seemed as exciting as having a grandmother who was dating an actor with a quintet of ex-wives.

She heard the doorbell, then her grandmother's voice. A minute later the kitchen door opened and Leila strolled in, followed by Lawrence. She was smartly dressed in pleated red slacks and a white, military-style blouse. Lawrence's navy blue cotton shirt and white slacks made him look as if he had just stepped off the cover of a men's fashion magazine.

Why didn't the man look his age? Silvey wondered in awe. Or at least show signs of a dissipated life?

With a flush of guilt, she shook off the thought, reminding herself not to be judgmental. She wanted to be open-minded about this new relationship of her grandmother's. She flashed Lawrence a cautious smile and the wary look in his eyes disappeared. "Good morning."

"Good morning," he boomed in his rich baritone. "I invited myself to breakfast."

Leila blessed them both with a delighted smile and immediately began rummaging in the refrigerator. Lawrence wanted bacon and eggs, but Leila gave him an appalled look. "Don't be ridiculous. A man of your age doesn't need all that cholesterol. Sit down. You're having melon and whole grain cereal with skim milk."

Silvey watched in amazement when he shrugged good-naturedly, sat down, and picked up the paper. She stared from one to the other of them, stunned. Not only was one of the world's greatest living actors sitting at their kitchen table, but he was meekly taking orders from her grandmother. Silvey put her hand to her chest. If she wasn't careful, she would hyperventilate. This was more than any normal woman should be expected to stand! She took a deep breath and then a sip of coffee.

After she recovered from her initial shock, Silvey began noticing how sweet the two of them were together. They talked and argued over the day's headlines as they ate cool green slices of honeydew melon, then kissed and made up over the cereal. It occurred to her that her grandmother could be very good for this man. She didn't kowtow or simper. She was a mature woman with definite ideas of her own.

Busy with her own thoughts, she didn't snap to attention until she heard Dan's name mentioned.

"The boy won't listen to me," Lawrence was saying as he sipped his coffee. "I keep telling him that nobody's going to take advantage of me, least of all you, but he insists I don't know what's good for me."

Silvey tapped her fingernails on the tabletop, thinking resentfully of his overbearing son.

"He's probably in shock," Leila soothed. "Give him time."

"I don't have time. I want to get things smoothed over with him before I go back to Los Angeles next month. I'll need all my concentration for a damned difficult part in that new miniseries. Besides, life is too short to spend it at odds with my only flesh and blood. I made enough of a hash of his life when he was young. We were estranged for years. I can't let it happen again."

Leila nodded sympathetically. "I would try to talk to him, but he certainly wouldn't listen to me."

The two of them fell silent and Silvey took the opportunity to introduce a topic of her own. "Mr. Wisdom, Lawrence...sir. About that loan...?"

He brightened immediately and his big hand came across the table to squeeze her forearm warmly. "You don't have to thank me. I was glad to do it. Gives me pleasure to do something with my money besides send it to ex-wives who use it to buy the skins of endangered animals." His eyes glimmered. "I want to do this for Leila. She's concerned about your future, your security."

Dismayed, Silvey looked from one to the other. If he was conning her, he was doing a great job of it. How could she refuse the loan? It meant so much to Grandma. "But your son seems so...."

"He loves me, though God knows I don't deserve it." Lawrence's craggy face eased into a smile. "Last year after my divorce, when I moved here, I was an emotional wreck." He cast a quick glance at Leila, who was smiling sympathetically. "Dan picked up the pieces and we became close, finally. I was wrong in not telling him about meeting Leila, but he was away and I knew he would be afraid I was getting myself into trouble."

No kidding, Silvey thought, propping her chin on her palm.

"He's angry now, as he has a right to be—and worried, but I don't seem to be able to find the words to ease his mind."

Engrossed in her own thoughts about Dan, it took Silvey a minute to realize the two of them had fallen silent and were staring at her expectantly. Wary brown eyes flew from one to the other of them. "What are you two thinking?"

Lawrence answered suavely, "That you're young, lovely...."

"And a perfect sacrificial lamb," she finished for him. "Oh, no... no. Just get that idea right out of your heads." She lifted her hands defensively.

"They stopped throwing young women into erupting volcanoes years ago."

"He might listen to you," Leila argued.

"Me? He hates me. He called me a...well, never mind what he called me," she muttered. "He won't listen to me."

"Please, honey. Try. Do it for me."

Dismayed, Silvey met Leila's pleading eyes. She knew her grandmother would have done anything for her. After a moment, she gulped. "All right. I'll try." They beamed at her with gratitude and approval, but she had a feeling she knew just how the biblical Daniel had felt when entering the lion's den.

Silvey thanked the student who had directed her to Dan's office and started down the hallway of the Sonora College office building. All the way over, she had worked on her little speech. For once, she was going to be ruled by her head rather than her heart.

She was going to be calm and reasonable when she talked to Dan. On the drive over, she thought about what kind of man he was. Protective, certainly, at least of his father. Direct. She'd had no doubt about what he thought of her and her grandmother. Although what he'd said still stung, she was trying to put it in perspective.

Someone was coming down the hall, and for a moment, she thought it was Dan. When he drew closer, she saw that it was a man with a slight build and dark, Latin eyes.

She looked, blinked, and stopped in her tracks. "John! John Ramos!"

He stopped, gazing with a perplexed frown at the woman whose face was wreathed in smiles. Frowning, he studied her features.

Her smile was growing impatiently expectant when light dawned in his eyes. "Silvey! What are you doing here?" He swooped forward and gathered her into his arms for a bear hug. "I haven't seen you since high school."

Happily, Silvey linked her hands with his and ran through a description of all that had happened to her. "And now I'm buying my own business," she concluded breathlessly. "What about you?"

John grinned. "You always could fit more words into a shorter space of time than anyone I ever knew. What have I been doing? Teaching high school history. Now I'm getting my doctorate here and working as a teaching assistant."

"Are you married?"

His handsome features creased in a grimace. "Married and divorced. Twice."

"Good grief, and you're not even thirty. You're going to wear yourself out!"

"Silvey, the amount of money I pay in support to my former spouses will wear me out long before any woman does. Besides, it's your fault, you know. I never recovered after you turned me down for the senior prom."

She waved that away. "Excuses, excuses. The truth was, I knew all about your reputation with girls."

"Oh, what was that?"

"That you had more hands than a battleship."

The two of them laughed together and John reached out to give her another hug. Caught off balance, Silvey turned her head away and came face to face with Dan Wisdom.

Her breath seesawed in and her eyes widened. She had completely forgotten about him. "Oh," she said weakly. "Hello."

"Am I interrupting something?" he asked in a cool tone. He let his gaze drift down to where John's arm clasped Silvey's waist, then back up to her reddening face.

She twisted out of John's arms, then berated herself for reacting so defensively. John, still grinning, let her go.

"Hi, Dan. Didn't know anyone was still around," he said. "Sorry if we disturbed you."

Silvey said, "I'm here to see Dr., uh . . . Dan."

John looked at Dan's less-than-welcoming expression. "Oh, I see." His friendliness faded as he gave Silvey a quick, assessing glance and stepped back. "Well, I won't keep you. Hey, Silvey, I'll give you a call, hmm?"

"Sure, John," she answered weakly as he walked away.

"The apple doesn't fall far from the tree, does it?" Dan observed.

She lifted her chin and her full mouth pinched into a tight line. "I beg your pardon?"

"Like grandmother, like granddaughter. Do you chase every man you meet?"

Anger spurted up, making her almost incoherent with rage. "John Ramos is an old high school friend of mine. We were gymnasts together. We . . . we had routines . . . and . . ."

"Yeah, I just saw one of your routines." He turned and started down the hallway. "If you're here to see me, come into my office."

He seemed to expect her to follow like a faithful pup. She crossed her arms over her chest and stood as if her shoes were glued to the carpet.

When he realized she wasn't following, he paused and looked back over his shoulder. "Something wrong?"

"*You're* wrong, Dr. Wisdom," she said, advancing on him. "I came here to reason with you. I didn't come to be insulted."

At first, Dan's expression didn't change as he gauged the determination in her face. He inclined his head as if he was giving in to her, though they both knew he was doing no such thing. "I apologize. Now can we conduct our business in my office?" He indicated a door.

Mollified, if not satisfied, Silvey graced him with a regal nod. "All right." It would take an effort, but she was woman enough to ignore his nasty personality and control her temper. She gave him a sideways glance, wishing hypocritically that he had inherited some of his father's charm.

She preceded him into his office with the irritated thought that today he looked like her idea of a college professor. She had never been to college, so she realized her expectations of how they dressed probably had no basis in reality, but she admitted that he looked respectable. He was wearing khaki slacks, a white shirt, a dark tie of muted design, and a summer jacket of lightweight fabric.

His change in clothing made her look at him as a person rather than an irritation. She glanced around with interest because she loved to see the kinds of things with which people surrounded themselves. It gave her insight into their personalities. From what she'd seen of Dan's personality so far, she could use some insight.

Inside, she scanned the walls decorated with carefully framed diplomas and photographs. One wall held a bookcase full of volumes.

A familiar cover caught her eye and she smiled. She reached over to pull the volume from the bookcase, thrilled that here was something the two of them could talk about without arguing. "Oh, you like D.K. Wilinson's books? I do, too, though I wasn't sure about the first one." She looked up with a small laugh. "I mean, really, a murder mystery set in pre-Colombian America? Who would have guessed it would be so exciting? The plot was especially surprising since the mystery was set in a society that practiced human sacrifice. The whole explanation for that and how it was different in their minds from actual murder was fascinating, but horrifying...."

She glanced up and her impulsive words skipped to a stop. His face was watchful, his head tilted as if he was listening carefully.

Silvey gave him a faint smile. "Sorry, I get a little carried away." She flipped the book's dust jacket open and went very still as she gazed at the solemn face of the author on the inside photograph.

"You're him," she said, her heart sinking as she stared at the photograph, then at him. "Wilinson is your pen name."

He nodded. "That's right, although I don't publicize it much."

"Why not?" Silvey replaced the volume. "This was on the bestseller list for weeks. I'd think you'd be proud of that."

"I am proud of it, of all my books, but I'm not interested in publicity. The money comes in handy. It goes to pay for my archaeological interests." He indicated the area behind her.

Silvey turned and her mouth dropped open.

From floor to ceiling, glass cases were filled with pottery, baskets, and artifacts. Her eyes darted over rare kachina dolls that represented Hopi gods, Hohokam and Anasazi pottery that might have been a thousand years old, metates used for grinding corn, and a dozen other items that could have come from only one source—Native American graves.

She whirled on him, her eyes full of accusation, her small chin as belligerent as a warrior's spear. "Just what kind of doctor are you?"

He drew back, frowning. "Cultural anthropology. Why?"

"Why the artifacts?"

"As I said, archaeology is an interest of mine, too. It's the same idea as anthropology except that the people are no longer around to give a verbal record."

"And Sonora College just happens to be trying to get government permission to excavate the ancient burial grounds of the Moreno Indians, right? You wouldn't be the one petitioning, would you?"

He nodded slowly, his eyes touching on the color pinkening the tip of her nose. "That bothers you?"

"Yes, it does. In my opinion, you're nothing but a glorified grave robber."

CHAPTER THREE

DAN'S chin drew back and his eyes glittered at her. "Don't tell me you're one of those people who think the past should stay buried? That we shouldn't try to learn from it?"

"I think my ancestors should stay buried. They have a right to rest in peace on their sacred mountain."

"*Your* ancestors?"

"That's right. My grandfather was descended from the Moreno Indians."

"Then you should want your children to know about the people from whom they're descended."

"I don't have any children."

"Yet." He folded his arms triumphantly.

Silvey did the same, matching him stance for stance, glare for glare. "There are federal laws prohibiting such excavations," she noted, anger flushing her cheeks with color.

"If the site is threatened by environmental damage or possible theft. . . ."

"Isn't that what we're talking about here?" Silvey interrupted sweetly, but he ignored her and went on.

"Permission can be granted to excavate."

"You have no right to dig people up, destroying what was precious to a tribe."

"It's an extinct tribe," he countered, his blue eyes bright and steady.

"Yes, the tribe has long since melted into others, but there are people, like me, who don't want the tribe's memories desecrated." Leila and her feisty friends, to name a few. They had recently discovered the plan to excavate the ancient site, and Silvey stood firmly with them against it. She decided instantly that she wouldn't tell Leila that Lawrence's son was in charge of the desecration. Of course, Leila might already know and hadn't mentioned it, not wanting to spoil her budding romance with Lawrence.

Leila. Lawrence.

With a sinking heart, she realized she had just antagonized the person she was supposed to be sweet talking. Her mind scrambled for a way out of this argument, but Dan had the bit between his teeth and was forging ahead.

The clean angles of his face worked as he talked. "Would you rather have real graverobbers up there? The only reason the site on Branaman Mountain has been safe so far is because the government has had a missile tracking station in the foothills. With military personnel crawling all over, there hasn't been much danger of thieves."

She gave him an evasive look. Darn it, why hadn't she stopped to think before she spoke? The last thing she needed was to antagonize the man further. "Well, now, I don't know...."

That was all he needed to be off and running again. "That's just the point. You *don't* know if anything has been disturbed. You'll never fully know until it's excavated, carefully studied. My team and I are the ones to do the job." He dragged a hand through his hair and glared at her in frustration.

She licked dry lips that felt as if she had powdered them with sandpaper. "Well, that's all very interesting, but it's not why I'm here."

He stared. "You brought it up!"

She answered with a sickly smile, but didn't reply.

A sigh gusted from between his tight lips. "All right. Why are you here, if not to be a soapbox sermonizer?"

"Mind if I sit down?" she asked, forming a conciliatory smile.

He stared at her for several seconds. The need to make his point warred with curiosity.

"Be my guest," he finally muttered, indicating the chair opposite his desk. He perched on the corner of the desk itself.

She sat and clasped her hands together in her lap, then consciously relaxed them. "The truth is, I came to say you were right. The money to buy my shop did come from your father." He stirred, but she held up her hands. "It's not what you think, though. It's merely a loan. We intend to sign a legally binding agreement detailing the exact terms of repayment." They hadn't actually talked about that yet, but it sounded good. "I'm a good manager, a good salesperson. I can make a success of the yogurt shop."

"You seem very sure of yourself."

"I am." Conviction rang in her voice.

His head tilted. "Tell me about your plans."

Silvey tried to relax in her chair. This was going better than she had expected, considering her opening gaffe. She launched into an account of past and projected sales, her experience and employees. Enthusiasm laced every word.

As he listened, the tension in Dan's shoulders eased. "Sounds like you've done your homework."

"Well, of course. It'll be my livelihood. I'm willing to work as hard as possible to make the shop a success. I think it could do a much larger volume of business than it's doing now." She launched into another enthusiastic lecture until Dan lifted his hands helplessly.

"All right, all right. I believe you." His lips twitched and then, as if he'd given himself permission to be pleasant, he relaxed and smiled.

Silvey grinned back. She recalled the passing thought she'd had the night before that he was actually quite good-looking. He was guarded, though, as if he had to monitor the emotions that he showed. One thing he couldn't hide, though, was his intensity. From what she had seen, he was a man strong in his beliefs and in the actions that went with those beliefs.

"What about your parents? And your grandmother? Don't they think you're a little young to be going into business for yourself?"

Silvey shrugged. "I've basically been on my own since I was eighteen. They trust me to know what I'm doing."

"I wish I did," he murmured.

Silvey bit back a sigh. "I'll simply have to prove myself, won't I?"

"Yes."

"And you'll expect Grandma to do the same thing."

"I can't deny that."

"I can see why you would be upset and worried, but my grandmother isn't some brainless bimbo who's after Lawrence's money. Once you get to know her, you'll see that."

Dan stared at her for a few more seconds before his momentary softening disappeared and he said, "I'll do that. In fact, I'll start tonight. The four of us will go somewhere together so I can get to know your grandmother."

Taken aback by his sudden decision, Silvey stammered, "Tonight?"

"Do you have an objection to that?"

Reminding herself she was trying to get on his good side, Silvey said, "No, no. That...that sounds fine...."

"You'll find someone to close up your shop this evening?"

It wasn't a request. Ordinarily, Silvey would have bridled at his tone, but she thought of Leila's happiness and checked her irritation. "Yes, all right. I've got employees to do it tonight."

"Fine." He stood suddenly. "I'll call and make reservations. I assume my father is at your house?"

Recognizing his dismissive tone, Silvey stood, but placed her hand on the back of the chair. His sudden change in attitude almost made her feel dizzy. "Yes, he is."

"I'll arrange everything. We'll pick you and your grandmother up at seven." He reached for the phone. "Oh, and one other thing."

"What's that?" she asked cautiously.

"My father won't be loaning you the money for your shop, after all. I will."

She blinked at him. "I beg your pardon?"

"It will solve the entire problem if I make the loan."

"What problem?"

"The problem of owing money to my father."

"You think it's better if I owe it to you?"

"Yes, if what you say is true—that your grandmother's interest is in Lawrence himself, and not in his money."

Silvey gritted her teeth. "It's true, but I'm not sure I'd rather borrow from you. Besides, the money has already been deposited to my account."

He lifted one shoulder in a shrug, but his eyes were shrewd. "Then you'll simply have to withdraw it and return it to my father, won't you? That is, if you haven't already spent it."

"No," she said through her teeth. "I haven't spent it."

"Then my offer stands. Take it or leave it, Miss Carlton. It's the only deal you're going to get from the Wisdoms."

In spite of the heat of anger that was beginning to swirl through her, Silvey tried to remain calm and rational. If she lost her temper now, it could really mess things up for Grandma. And how could she argue if he insisted on making the loan? She couldn't very well say she'd rather have his father's money. It would only confirm what he already thought of the Carlton women. Besides, he'd probably argue right back that there were already plenty of women getting his father's money.

After several seconds of silence, Silvey nodded and held out her hand. "All right," she said. "It's a deal."

Dan took her hand in his and gave it a firm shake. Silvey drew away quickly even as her mind registered the fact that his hand was strong and tough, not what she would have expected from a man who made his living from behind a desk.

Everything about him was unexpected, she decided irritably. She couldn't quite read him because he kept her constantly off balance. She tried to sum him up in one sentence, but even when she strung together the words—overprotective son, cultural anthropologist turned archaeologist, mystery writer—well, it still didn't seem quite real.

Dan lifted an eyebrow at her. "Why are you staring at me like that?"

Silvey felt color touching her cheeks again, but she refused to let her gaze waver. "I was thinking that you're hard to read—to understand."

"And you want to understand me?"

The way he said it, with a touch of humor, made her feel foolish, but she lifted her chin and said, "Yes. Yes, I do. After all, you'll be holding the paper on my loan."

"That's true, but that doesn't mean we have to understand each other personally."

Silvey tilted her head as he spoke. There was something in his tone that she couldn't quite pin down. It sounded as if he was trying to keep her at arm's length. She wasn't accustomed to that kind of treatment from men. She'd had many boyfriends and even after the romance cooled, had remained on amiable terms with them. She couldn't recall ever meeting a man who was so thoroughly reluctant to get to know her.

His very reluctance piqued her and she said impishly, "I think we'll understand each other especially well if Grandma and Lawrence decide to marry."

Dan frowned ferociously as she crossed her arm over her waist, propped her chin on her fingertip, and said thoughtfully, "That would make you, what? My step uncle?"

Dan looked appalled. "Hardly likely. I'll do my best to see they don't marry."

"You may not be able to stop them."

His blue eyes darkened to a shade close to midnight. "We'll see. In the meantime, don't you encourage them."

From what she'd seen, the two of them didn't need any encouragement! Silvey refrained from pointing that out. Why make Dan any more antagonistic than he already was? She nodded agreeably.

Seeing he had her somewhat reluctant acquiescence, Dan said, "I'll need to see a report of projected costs for your shop. Then I'll have the contract drawn up."

It took her a few seconds to catch up with his change of topic. "Projected costs? Oh, oh, of course," she answered, trying to sound businesslike. "I'll do that right away."

Dan slipped from the desk and looked down at her. "In the meantime, I'll see you tonight."

Silvey's head was spinning. Dazed, she touched her fingertips to her forehead even as she turned toward the door. "Tonight. Seven o'clock. What should I wear?"

Dan opened his office door for her and once again she saw that quick, rare smile of his, as if their moment of disagreement had only been an illusion. "Your dancing shoes."

"Something tells me this isn't going to be a regular Friday night date," Silvey murmured as she stared out her front door at the two men coming up the steps.

When she and Dan had made the arrangements that morning, she hadn't expected him and Lawrence to arrive in a vintage Silver Cloud Rolls-Royce that boasted acres of gleaming paint and miles of blinding chrome. As if that wasn't enough of a shock, the two men were dressed in white dinner jackets.

Dan correctly read the stunned look on her face when he caught sight of her in the open doorway. "Dad insisted," he said, indicating the jacket and the knife-creased black slacks.

"Oh, I see," she answered weakly, her gaze flying up to take in his handsomeness. His shoulders looked twice as broad, his waist half its width in the beautifully cut jacket. The angles of his freshly shaven jaw all but glistened in the dying sunlight. The subtle, musky scent of his cologne teased her senses and fluttered at her heart.

She had a hard time remembering just why she'd disliked him so much the night before, but she recalled quite vividly what she'd found so attractive about him that morning.

"Silvey, why don't you ask them in?" Leila chided, her tone amused.

Embarrassed that she'd been standing and staring at Dan, Silvey stepped back hastily, color washing into her cheeks. "Of course. Please come in."

Once inside, Lawrence and Leila gave each other approving compliments and warm hugs. Silvey thought with satisfaction that her grandmother looked fabulous in a smart red evening suit with sequins scattered across the lapels.

Dan observed them with a slight frown, then turned to Silvey. "I hope this was a good idea." His gaze swept over her short jade green satin dress with a cinched waist and flared skirt, then up to her hair. Trying for sophistication, she had pulled her shoulder-length hair into a cascade of curls at the back of her head. "I guess it was," he murmured approvingly.

Silvey felt as if the floor had been cut away from beneath her feet. Again, he had surprised her, and she had to admit that she was thrilled by his approval.

"Are we ready to go?" Lawrence asked in his forceful voice, breaking into Silvey and Dan's absorption with each other. They both stepped back, blinking as if they'd come out of a dark cave.

"Of course," Silvey answered on a rush of breath. She didn't let her gaze meet Dan's again as she and Leila made preparations to leave, finding their small evening bags and checking the contents.

They locked the house and walked to the Rolls-Royce. Silvey thought they made quite a show for the neighbors, who were gathering on their lawns, hoses and sprinklers at hand in a pretense of flower-watering. She and Leila grinned and waved cheerfully as they seated themselves sedately in the car.

Once settled into the backseat with Dan, Silvey gazed at the luxurious interior which was white leather and burgundy satin with touches of gold trim that she could have sworn was real. On each door frame was an ornate bud vase holding a dewy-fresh white rose.

For the first time, Silvey took a mental step back from herself and considered just what kind of world she and her grandmother had stumbled into. Up until now she had been concentrating on keeping her mental balance in everything that had happened in the past twenty-four hours. Looking around, she realized that she and Leila were in a far different world than their usual, very ordinary one.

It was true that money could make a big difference in a person's life-style, but for all his wealth, she knew that Lawrence had never been a particularly happy man.

What about Dan? His alter ego as D.K. Wilinson must keep him financially well-fixed if he was able to use the income to pay for his archaeological interests. But was he happy?

Reaching out, she touched the gold trim edging the door. It even felt expensive.

She glanced up to see Dan watching her. Self-consciously, she drew her hand away and folded her fingers together in her lap.

"Yes, it's real," he said, drawing her attention back to him.

"You mean the trim? Isn't Lawrence afraid of thieves?"

"He rarely drives this car."

"Then what's the point of owning it?"

"Thinking it would bring in quite a nice profit if he sold it?"

A sharp retort sprang to her lips, but she bit it back, aware of Leila and Lawrence in the front seat. She forced her jaw to relax as she said, "I suppose you can think that if you choose."

Dan's eyes narrowed at her cool tone. "I suppose I can—at least until I find out differently."

Silvey looked into his eyes, wishing there was something she could say or do to change his opinion of her...and of Leila, but it wouldn't be easy. There were reserves of determination in this man that she could only guess at.

Practicing a little determination of her own, she pulled her mind away from disturbing thoughts and gave him an appreciative look.

She studied his elegant profile, the perfect cut of his dinner jacket. She'd *never* before been out with a man in a dinner jacket, although she admitted it was something she could probably get used to very quickly.

Glancing down, she touched the skirt of her dress. She had bought it slightly damaged on clearance sale at an upscale department store. It was beautiful, but she suddenly felt self-conscious as her fingers sought out the almost invisible repair of the tiny hole near the hem. Something about knowing it was there made her feel as if she was out of place.

When Dan gave her a questioning glance, she realized she was crumpling the fabric. She forced her hands to relax and let her spine rest against the plush seat. This was just one evening out of her life, after all. It wasn't as if she'd be dressing like this and riding around in a Rolls every day.

Silvey's thoughts were interrupted by Lawrence, who launched into a story about the time he had gone on a driving vacation through Mexico. Dan, then twelve, had gone along and their adventures sounded like an old Laurel and Hardy film.

"Actually, it all went pretty well," Dan admitted. "That is, until some of the women in one little village recognized Dad and started throwing themselves at him, begging for autographs. While he was busy getting writer's cramp, I went off and stumbled across my first archaeological dig—a group from a university in Mexico City."

"Were they looking for Aztec artifacts?"

He nodded, his eyes flashing in eagerness that was both boyish and masculine. "While I was watching, they found a gold medallion. Very small, but perfect." His grin flickered. "I was hooked."

Silvey gave him a curious look as Lawrence and Leila became absorbed in a conversation of their own. "And what about you? Have you personally found anything of historical significance?"

"Not yet." He leaned back in the seat and stretched one arm along the plush back as he answered in a low tone, "Maybe I'll make my big discovery on Branaman Mountain."

"Then again, maybe you won't."

Challenge lightened his eyes and he leaned close to her. "Why don't we wait and see?"

"Why don't we?"

She'd had the last word, but when he chuckled deep in his throat, she knew she hadn't won the skirmish.

She looked away and was glad when they pulled up outside a restaurant which specialized in international cuisine.

As they walked inside, Silvey could only look around in awed pleasure at the dark-paneled walls, the heavy damask tablecloths, bone china and sterling silver. She didn't know about Leila, but this place was by far the nicest restaurant she'd ever been in. She sincerely hoped she didn't disgrace herself.

When she caught Dan looking at her, she lifted her chin and sailed along behind the maître d' as he showed them to their table in a secluded alcove.

Their dinner would be wonderful and fabulously expensive. Silvey could barely keep from gasping aloud when she opened her menu and saw the prices printed inside.

Once their orders had been placed, Silvey sipped cautiously at a glass of wine and listened to the conversation between the other three at the table.

Dan asked Leila about her background in the circus and about her work as a social activist. Silvey relaxed until she realized that his questions were much more pointed and went much deeper than polite interest.

She sat forward and gave him a straight look as she spoke to his father. "So, Lawrence, tell us about the role you'll have in the miniseries."

Before Lawrence could open his mouth, Dan answered, "Dad doesn't like to discuss his roles before shooting actually begins. Says it saps his creativity. Tell me, Leila, what got you interested in being an activist? You've had a busy life. Don't you feel that you deserve to take things easy?"

Irritated, Silvey said, "Grandma says staying busy watching out for others keeps her young."

"Well, it certainly seems to be working," Dan observed.

Leila treated him to a coy smile. Lawrence beamed approvingly. As the two of them gazed into each other's eyes, Silvey wrinkled her nose as if she'd caught a whiff of something rotten.

Dan's eyes glittered at her over the rim of his wineglass.

Silvey smirked and he coughed as if the wine had gone down the wrong way. Inwardly, she fumed at his pointed tactics and she desperately wanted to tell him what she thought of him.

Their food arrived at that moment and she was saved from blurting out something she might regret. She contented herself with a warning glance, which Dan greeted with complete innocence.

She calmed down enough to enjoy her delicious dinner, but she vowed she would discuss this with him later. When they prepared to leave, Dan withdrew his checkbook to pay for their meal. Silvey deliberately swept her evening bag from her lap. On the pretext of picking it up, she leaned close to Dan and gave his checkbook a thorough enough glance to memorize his phone number. He gave her a curious look, but she merely smiled.

Two could play at this innocence game.

CHAPTER FOUR

UNHURRIEDLY, they drove home and when they reached the house, Leila and Lawrence seemed to want a few moments alone. Silvey felt inclined to linger, but this time it was Dan who pointed out that the older couple might like some privacy. He helped her from the car and she walked, back straight, to her front porch. She pulled her key out and Dan took it from her to unlock the front door.

"Aren't you afraid your spine will snap, holding it so stiff like that?" he asked, bending slightly from the waist to give her back a considering look.

"Aren't you afraid you'll get a reputation for being two-faced?" she countered.

"Why would I?"

"I thought you were going to give her the benefit of the doubt, but you were positively *grilling* my grandmother. It wouldn't have surprised me if you'd whipped out hot lights and a one-way mirror."

"You're exaggerating," he scoffed. "I was taking a polite interest in her activities."

"Polite," she sputtered, tossing her head back so hard that a few of her curls slipped loose from their anchorage. Distracted, she shoved them back into place. "Polite is not the word."

"And I'll bet you've got just the word for it."

"Yes. Judgmental." More curls fell and she lifted both hands to fix them.

With an indulgent smile, Dan gently, but firmly, pulled her arms down. With deft movements of his fingers, he pulled out pins, wound up curls, and set them back in place.

Taken aback, Silvey could only stare for a few seconds before she recovered enough to slap his hands away. "Stop that! I can take care of my own hair, thank you very much."

In an expansive gesture, he spread his arms wide and said, "Whatever you say, Miss Carlton."

Silvey frowned. How could she argue with someone who was so outwardly agreeable? She was trying to get back to the point she was making when Lawrence alighted from the car, smoothed his mussed hair, straightened his bow tie, which had somehow become skewed beneath his right ear, and walked around to help Leila out.

The older couple drifted up the walk and Silvey had to file away the pungent remarks she had for Dan. He gave her a knowing grin as he told her good-night, gave Leila a courtly salute and accompanied his father back to the car.

Once they were inside, Leila commented dreamily on how well the evening had gone and floated away to her room.

Fuming, Silvey paced the floor until she thought Dan had sufficient time to reach home—she'd memorized the address, too—then she pounced on the phone, rapidly punching out his number.

When Dan answered, she blurted, "You were grilling her."

Dan was silent when he recognized her voice but when he spoke, she was sure he was grinning.

"Good evening to you, too, Silvey. Didn't we just say goodbye?"

"Don't try to change the subject."

"And what was the subject?"

"Your questions tonight."

"And what was wrong with them?" he asked reasonably.

"You . . . you were only trying to find out the negative things about her. You didn't focus on the positive at all." Silvey prowled restlessly around the room, her satin dress keeping up a whispered accompaniment as she moved, carrying the phone with her.

"Then tell me the positive." His voice, coming over the wire, was low and seductive. Unexpectedly, goose bumps rose on Silvey's arms. Refusing to believe it was caused by anything except the air-conditioning, she dragged the phone with her as she adjusted the thermostat upward.

"She's loving and generous," Silvey said, frowning at the temperature control. "She's genuinely concerned about other people and she likes doing things to help them."

"I see."

"You do?" she asked suspiciously. Some of the stiffness began easing from her shoulders. She seated herself on the arm of the sofa.

"Yes, but you need to explain more."

Warily, Silvey said, "Leila says it's the duty of every able-bodied person to help those less fortunate."

"Hmm, that sounds reasonable."

"Do you think so?" Silvey slipped her high heels off and wiggled her toes.

"Absolutely. Tell me more."

Pleased and surprised by his receptiveness, Silvey slid off the sofa arm onto the seat. "That's why she started her group of activists—to help others." She placed her stockinged feet on the coffee table and leaned back. "Since the activists—they call themselves Leila's Warriors—are all retired, they've got time to pursue important social reforms."

"Like better health care for the elderly?"

Silvey leaned against the arm of the sofa and propped her elbow on a cushion. Sliding onto her spine, she was almost prone. "That and better conditions in nursing homes. Why, you'd be shocked at how poorly some of them are operated."

"I'm sure I would," Dan said.

Mollified by his agreeability, Silvey let her head fall back and her eyes drift shut as she concentrated on his voice. Strange how she'd felt tense all day, either when with him, thinking about him, or anticipating their double date. Now, on the phone with him, she was able to relax for the first time since waking up that morning.

"What about you, Silvey?" Dan went on.

"What about me?"

"Are you interested in all those causes that your grandmother is involved in?"

"Well, yes. Yes, I am. Some of them, at least."

"I thought so, especially the Branaman Mountain excavation."

"Of course. It involves my ancestors. My family."

"And you're very loyal to them."

"Certainly," she said, trying to sound as loyal as a troop of army veterans.

"Mmm," he murmured in a tone that shimmied delight from vertebra to vertebra, hopscotching all the way up her backbone. She closed her eyes to shut out distractions and better concentrate on the strangely pleasant sensations his voice was evoking.

"What you're saying is that your grandmother is open with her time, and generous with her love and concern for others?"

"Exactly."

"Well, I have just one thing to say to that, Silvey."

"What's that?"

"She sounds exactly like you."

Silvey's eyes sprang open and she sat up. "A compliment?"

"Sounded suspiciously like one, didn't it?"

"Yes."

"I'll have to be careful."

"You'd better. That kind of thing can go to a girl's head."

He chuckled. "In that case, I'd better concentrate on your feet."

"I beg your pardon?" She frowned at the unromantic comment, then wondered why she was thinking in terms of romance when it was crystal clear that was something neither of them wanted.

"I told you to wear your dancing shoes tonight, but I didn't take you dancing."

Silvey smiled and found herself caressing the receiver. "And you're a man of your word."

"So I've been told," he said modestly.

Silvey couldn't suppress a giggle. "I can't let you break your word."

"No, you can't. We'll go dancing tomorrow night. You can sing Leila's praises to me some more."

"I'll do that."

"I'll see you tomorrow night at eight, then."

"All right, Dan." Silvey told him good-night, placed the receiver on its hook, then sat staring into space trying to pinpoint the exact moment when her irritation with him had turned into eager anticipation to see him again.

Thoughtfully, Silvey rubbed her chin.

How had that happened, anyway? She distinctly remembered being thoroughly irritated with him at the beginning of the conversation, but he had turned the tables on her so that she had been all but purring by the time she had hung up the phone. She'd even accepted a date with him, this time without her grandmother's presence.

Silvey frowned. This might not be such a good idea, after all. It was one thing to have Leila and Lawrence along, and for the older couple to be the focus between her and Dan. But tomorrow night, even if she did, indeed, sing Leila's praises to him, she would be alone with him while doing it.

Silvey wondered why he was taking her out again. Surely not to discuss the loan he was giving her—though that might come up during the evening.

Silvey sighed. She'd been suckered, blind-sided, thrown for a loop. Dan had told her exactly what he really wanted—to hear more about Leila, but he was still suspicious of both Silvey and Leila. He couldn't believe Leila was as unselfish as she seemed.

Jumping to her feet, Silvey stalked around the room. He couldn't get Leila alone to examine her motives. Lawrence wouldn't stand for it. But he could get Silvey alone. With a grimace, Silvey admitted that it didn't help that she was so enthralled with him—and that it showed. If she was going to protect Leila's interests, and her own, Silvey knew she was going to have to be as wily as Dan. Oh, yes, she would go out with him again, but she'd be careful about what she said and about how she reacted to what Dan said.

The next night found them once again in the Rolls, heading off into the night. This time, Dan was driving. Lawrence had insisted that they take the car. He had dropped by to spend the evening with Leila, bringing with him a few videos of his favorite movies. Silvey had been amused to note that he was the star in all of them. She and Dan had left the older couple popping popcorn in the microwave and flipping the tops open on cans of soda.

As Silvey and Dan pulled away from the curb in the magnificent automobile, she nervously smoothed the skirt of her yellow silk sheath. She knew she looked good. The dress had matching heels that added three inches to her height and, once again, she'd wound her hair into a sleek French roll, but tonight, she'd used more hairpins. She could only hope that her appearance hid the fact that her nerves were sizzling with anticipation.

Dan said, "Dad tells me the El Monte Hotel ballroom has an honest-to-goodness dance band that plays tunes from the forties and fifties."

Surprised, she turned to him. "You'd rather go there than to a club?"

"If you don't mind. Clubs are too noisy."

Silvey rested her forearm across her waist and her chin on her fingertips. "And you want to be able to talk, to ask me about Leila?"

Dan slid her a sideways glance. "That's right. Besides, I'm better at the old-fashioned two-step and the foxtrot than I am at modern dances."

"Why's that?"

"My dad was a party animal during my formative years. I could cha-cha and samba long before I could disco. Dad had a cast party for every movie he made. In fact, he had a party for any excuse he could think of."

"Didn't you ever want to hide or be alone during these parties?"

"Sure." Dan shrugged. "I had the normal teenage aversion to contact with anyone over thirty, but it didn't do any good to hide. They'd come find me and insist that I join in."

Silvey smiled, but she couldn't help being disturbed by the mental image of Dan, a solitary boy, trying to grow up in the middle of endless rounds of parties and excitement. She wondered if that kind of upbringing had contributed to his present choice of careers. In academic pursuits and in writing fiction, he probably needed long periods of deep concentration and quiet—something his growing up years had lacked.

And where had his mother been during all of this? she wondered, incensed. Dan talked as though he'd lived alone with his father and string of stepmothers, never mentioning his own mother.

Silvey shivered as she wondered what kind of relationship Dan had maintained with his mother, and what kind of attitude toward women he'd developed from seeing Lawrence's example. She could guess, though, having been faced with Dan's suspicions about her and Leila's motives.

When they reached the El Monte, they found a table at the edge of the dance floor. Before they were even seated, Dan tilted his head toward the crowd of dancers. Most of them were older, but Silvey was surprised to see that there were many young couples, too. "Care to join them?" he said.

Silvey's eyes lit like summer lightening. She loved dancing. Her feet were fairly itching to get out there. "I'd love to. After all, that's why we came—that, and to make sure you remain a man of your word."

"Ah, yes, and you were going to tell me more about your grandmother's sterling qualities."

"That's right."

She gave him an insincere smile. "Mustn't forget why we're here. Although, in my opinion, we could have had this talk while sitting on my front porch."

"Maybe we should have," he said, taking her hand. "That way I could have kept an eye on Dad and Leila."

Silvey rolled her eyes. "They don't need you watching over them."

"I don't know about that." After a moment, he added reflectively, "Dad's in an odd mood tonight."

"Why do you say that?"

"Because he insisted we take the Rolls. He doesn't usually do that because he's very protective of it."

"Maybe he's just happy to be with Grandma," she suggested brightly. "Without you breathing down his neck."

"Maybe."

"You're a hard man to convince," Silvey said in a long-suffering tone.

Dan took her into his arms and moved her onto the polished wooden floor.

The band was playing an old Glenn Miller tune, "String of Pearls." A huge, reflective ball suspended from the middle of the ceiling rotated slowly. Lights shone on it, scattering pinpricks of brightness around the darkened room. The mood was romantic, yet mysterious.

Against her will, Silvey found herself getting caught up in that mood. Even though there were dozens of other couples in the room, Silvey felt as if she and Dan were alone. Moving with the flow of the music and the fluid grace of Dan's motions, she reminded herself not to relax too much. She had to stay mentally alert if she was going to deal with Dan.

"Now's your chance," he commanded. "Tell me more about your grandmother. And while you're at it, throw in a few incidentals about yourself."

"Gee," she murmured, glancing at him from beneath her lashes, "I don't know when I've been more flattered."

He gave her a pointed look to urge her along and she launched into a narrative about the years she and Leila had spent as circus acrobats. She described how her grandfather, who had been ringmaster and part owner of a circus, had wooed her grandmother and how they had stuck together through all the upheavals of their nomadic life. Her own father, Richard, hadn't liked the life, so when he'd married, he and Silvey's mother had lived in Tucson for Silvey's growing-up years. They'd taken jobs with an oil company when she had left to join her grandparents.

"Why didn't you stay with the circus?" Dan asked.

"I was more like my dad than I thought I was," she admitted ruefully. "I loved performing, but the nomadic life wasn't for me. I like having a real home."

Dan met her eyes but his voice was strangely flat. "Yes, having a real home can sound very attractive."

Nonplussed, Silvey blinked at the odd comment and couldn't think of anything to say.

"But your grandmother loved the circus life?" Dan went on.

"I don't know that she really loved it, but she loved my grandfather. They were married for forty-eight years. No one can say she gives up when the going gets tough."

The music changed to "Can't Help Lovin' That Man of Mine." Dan said, "I think the same could be said for you."

"I hope so."

"Either you're persevering or just plain stubborn."

Silvey grinned and batted her eyelashes at him. "You're the learned professor and famous writer. You choose the word that fits best."

"Stubborn," he decided.

She wrinkled her nose at him, then tilted her head back to look into his face. "You know, Dan, this whole situation would be much easier if you were selfish and unconcerned about your father."

"It would?"

"Yes, because then I could honestly dislike you for your suspicions about Leila's motives."

Dan looked down at her with narrowed eyes. "Do you *ever* have a thought you don't feel compelled to express?"

Heat rushed to Silvey's cheeks. "Occasionally."

"Rarely," Dan corrected. He drew her closer, his hand tightening on the small of her back. "At least you realize I'm worried about Dad."

Silvey had a quick retort ready to fly, but she suddenly became aware of the way Dan was holding her. A new, more dangerous tension transferred itself from his hand to the back of her waist. It sizzled through her, reminding her of the reaction she had felt the night before when they'd been talking on the phone. The only difference was that he was much more potent in person.

Her eyes shot up to his and she saw that he was watching her with wary interest. He released her fingers and dropped his hands to join together at her waist, drawing her to him until their lower bodies touched.

Tingling joy rippled through her. She didn't know how she kept dancing with her legs melted off below the knees.

Excitement started as a slow heat deep inside her. It was unexpected but not unwelcome. She usually made buddies of the men she met, but she couldn't see that happening with Dan. He was too driven

and intense, not to mention opinionated, to be
turned into a pal. Not that he had given much in-
dication he saw her as anything but a minor
character in this drama concerning his father.

A slow fire began to simmer in his eyes as he
looked at her. Speckles of light from the rotating,
reflective ball dappled his face and flashed in his
eyes. "You're a good dancer, Silvey."

"Comes from being an acrobat."

"Am I a better partner than that floor mop?"

Her gaze flew to his. He *had* been watching her
silly dance. She sniffed and gave him a superior
look. "At least your knees bend."

Dan laughed against her hair and Silvey smiled.
Their feet went through the automatic steps but they
were lost to the music and their surroundings.

Every one of her senses was open to the fullest.
She was sure she would never forget the music being
played, the feel of his arms around her, the rich
fabric of his jacket, the texture of his hair, his body
pressed against hers, the heady maleness of his
scent, the soft murmur of his voice.

Dan's smile matched hers as his gaze touched her
face, lingering on the awareness in her eyes. Heat
whooshed down Silvey's body, flipped her stomach
over a couple of times, and zipped back up like a
jet-propelled elevator.

She stumbled just as the dance was ending. Dan
caught her, gave her a knowing smile, and swept
her into the next number. They danced several more
dances, then sat at a table drinking coffee and
talking.

Silvey was surprised and delighted to discover
that they had a great deal in common besides their

concern for Lawrence and Leila. Given the tone of their initial meetings, Silvey never would have guessed they could talk for two hours without arguing. She was pleased, but still uncertain. She didn't know if she had accomplished her stated goal of changing his mind about Leila. By going out with Dan for the evening, she had also given Leila and Lawrence some time alone.

When they left the El Monte and drove home, she had second thoughts as soon as Leila and Lawrence met them at the door with glowing faces.

Silvey could feel Dan tensing even before Lawrence said, "Come on in, kids, we've got something important to discuss with you."

"What is it, Dad?" Dan asked, his tone cutting through the festive mood he and Silvey had enjoyed all evening.

Silvey met his gaze and shrugged to show she didn't know what it was about, either. She walked into the living room and sat down.

Leila fluttered about nervously, touching objects here and there, then grabbing Lawrence's hand and clinging to it. Silvey watched all this in growing alarm. As Dan came down beside Silvey on the sofa, he flicked open the button of his jacket and spread his arms along the back of the sofa. Silvey could see that although his pose was casual, his fingers dug into the polished cotton fabric. "All right, Dad," he said. "Shoot."

Lawrence looked suddenly tense as he eyed his son, but happiness still glowed from him. "Well, as you know, I've signed for a role in a miniseries. I got a call today saying production has been moved up due to cancelation of another project. I have to be on the set next week."

Dan's face cleared. "That's great, Dad. I . . ."

"I'm not finished," Lawrence said, holding up his hand. "We're going to be shooting in California and Mexico for several weeks. I don't want to be separated from Leila for that long, so I've asked her to accompany me."

Silvey jerked as if she'd had the breath knocked from her. For a second, she couldn't get it back and darkness threatened to close in at the corners of her eyes. Finally she gasped, "Accompany you? Exactly what does that mean?"

Leila broke in, "He's asked me to marry him."

Silvey gasped. Her old fears about Lawrence came sweeping back. The man had been married five times! "Gr-grandma, I . . . I . . ."

"You don't know what to say?" Leila asked, beaming up at Lawrence. "I didn't, either, when he asked me right in the middle of one of his movies. There he was on the screen, proposing to Bette Davis, and sitting on my sofa proposing to me." Her eyes grew misty. "It was very romantic."

"I'll bet," Silvey choked.

"Of course, when I got my breath back, I said yes before he changed his mind."

Her grandmother seemed oblivious to her distress. Silvey tried to get it under control, but failed. Her hands began to shake and she realized it was from anger. What could Grandma be thinking? Dating a man like Lawrence was one thing, but marriage! It didn't bear thinking about.

Through numb lips, Silvey asked, "When?"

"When will we be married, you mean?"

Lawrence interrupted. "Dan's worried that I might be rushing into things again, so we're going to make this a long engagement. That's why Leila's coming to California with me. Shooting my part in the miniseries will take five or six weeks and the studio has booked us a suite at the Beverly Hills Hotel for the duration."

A lump had formed in Silvey's throat and it grew bigger and bigger as she stared first at Lawrence, then Leila. Her grandmother was going to California to cohabitate with Lawrence Wisdom, and then marry him in a few weeks.

Unbelievable! How was she ever going to explain this to her dad?

Her dazed eyes swung to Dan, who hadn't moved a muscle or even seemed to breathe in several minutes. His face was pale, his brows were drawn together and the look in his eyes was terrible. His jaw was clenched as if he would like to take a bite out of something. He seemed to get himself under control with great effort, turned to her and said, "Can I speak to you in the kitchen for a minute, please?"

She shook her head. "I've got to talk to Grandma."

"In the kitchen now, please," he insisted, standing and grabbing her hand.

She resisted, pulling back from him, but he was having none of it. He tugged her to her feet and into the kitchen while Lawrence and Leila watched in surprise.

Once there, he shut the door and dragged her across the room. "I hope you didn't encourage this." His voice was hard and level.

Her brown eyes wide with shock, Silvey stared at him. "What?"

He paced a few steps across the kitchen, then circled back to her. "I said, I hope you didn't encourage this."

"Why on earth would you think that? I'm just as stunned as you are."

Dan pointed an accusing finger at her. "Yesterday morning you were telling me there was a chance they might marry."

Silvey threw her hands out. "I was *joking*! I didn't think they'd really do it, at least not this soon."

"Well, *I* was hoping they wouldn't do it at all!" Turning, he began pacing from the sink to the back door. "And you've done nothing to encourage them . . . ?"

"Weren't you listening?" she asked furiously. "I said that, haven't I? And I don't appreciate you accusing me." Turning, she began pacing, too, from the refrigerator to the table and back again.

He was impossible, she thought, completely impossible. She had been entertaining such romantic thoughts about him and now he was throwing accusations at her. He hadn't been kidding when he said they didn't need to understand each other, but it hurt to realize how strongly he'd meant it.

Meeting in the middle of the floor, they side-stepped each other pointedly and she gave him a furious look.

He arched a brow at her. "You can't blame me for what I'm thinking."

"I certainly can. You always think the worst of Grandma, and of me. I'd like to point out that it was your father who did the proposing—right in the middle of one of his old movies. She certainly didn't wrestle him to the ground and hold him prisoner until he promised to marry her!''

His lips drew together and he spun away, resuming his pacing. After a few more circuits, he stopped by the sink and curled his fingers over the edge. He stood like that for several seconds before he loosened his hands, turned his back to the sink and stood with his arms crossed over his chest, and his hands tucked up under his arms. Scowling fiercely, he watched her continue her own pacing.

When some of her anger and worry began to cool, her steps slowed.

At last, Dan spoke, his voice was as low and rough as rusty barbed wire. ''What are you thinking?''

Still stung by his accusation, she gave him a frosty look. ''Probably the same thing you are. That they're making a mistake.''

''Are you saying that all the good things you told me about Leila aren't true?''

''Of course they're true, but . . . but I was joking when I said you'd be my step uncle. I know they're attracted to each other . . . but marriage!''

''Right now, they're only engaged,'' he conceded.

''And on the verge of moving into a love nest at the Beverly Hills Hotel! Am I supposed to take comfort in that?''

They fell into another troubled silence. Dan lifted his chin from where it had been resting on his chest and stared at her. ''Do you think we can stop them?''

"No," she answered on a great sigh, pulling out a chair and sinking into it. She rested her forehead on her palm.

She watched Dan's troubled face and felt her own hurt and anger begin to dissipate. She shouldn't be so upset. She'd known from the moment they met that his first concern was his father. His accusation hurt because it showed how little he really knew about her, but it shouldn't surprise her.

Dan lifted his hands and ran them wearily over his face. "They'll do it with or without our approval, but I wish I could stop him."

"You said yesterday that you'd do your best to see they didn't marry. Does that still hold?"

Dan only looked at her from beneath his scowling brows.

She exhaled an exasperated breath. "And you say *I'm* stubborn! You'll only end up by being estranged from him. Is that what you want?"

"No."

"It's not what I want with Grandma, either."

Dan's face was anguished. "You don't know what it was like. That last divorce nearly killed him."

"*You* don't know what it was like. Five years ago, Grandma lost her husband and not long after that, she lost a job she'd held for almost fifty years. She was scared to death of not being needed, so she started her little group of activists. She has to have a cause to work for. I'm afraid she sees your father as someone to be rescued."

They were both silent, Dan leaning up against the counter, his arms folded and his thumb raking his chin, Silvey sitting across the room from him.

When she thought about how close they'd been earlier and how far apart they were now, the distance across the beige tile seemed limitless.

"Maybe that's not so bad," Dan ventured, catching her by surprise.

"What?"

"Dad needs someone to take care of him. Leila needs to care for someone." He shuddered. "But...another wife!"

Silvey drew in a deep breath. "At least he's not rushing into it this time."

"True," Dan conceded, but he didn't sound comforted.

"I realize you don't know her very well, but can you say, from what you've seen of her, that Grandma is anything like those other women?"

"God, no," he answered in a fervent tone.

"They'll probably get married in spite of our objections," Silvey said flatly. "So we might as well make it pleasant for them."

"Dad did promise a long engagement," he said in a thoughtful tone that made Silvey shift uncomfortably. A long engagement would give him more time to interfere.

"Yes, he did. They'll have more time to get to know each other. Believe me, if Lawrence gives Grandma any trouble, she'll hog-tie him and talk some sense into him," she said, forcing levity into her voice, even as it broke. She looked down at the floor and shook her head as tears formed. "I don't want him to hurt her, either."

"Then this is your chance to stop them."

Silvey shook her head. "I won't...can't...*we* can't tell them what to do."

Dan was silent for a moment. When he spoke, his voice was cool. "We'd better go back in."

She nodded, looking into his eyes, feeling despair at the momentary closeness that had slipped away from them.

He took her elbow and they walked back into the living room. She went to Leila and gave her a hug as she watched Dan.

"Congratulations, Dad," he said, reaching out to shake his father's hand.

Lawrence breathed a great sigh of relief and exchanged sparkling glances with Leila. Only Silvey saw the cold determination that filled Dan's eyes.

CHAPTER FIVE

"AND please don't forget to water my roses. You know how they burn up in the summer heat if they're not well watered."

Silvey nodded. "Yes, Grandma. I'll remember." She added a note to the growing list of things Leila wanted done while she was gone. Her grandmother could stay home and do all these things herself, Silvey thought grumpily, instead of cavorting off to California with Lawrence. In spite of the pep talk she and Dan had given each other two nights ago, she was still not reconciled to her grandmother's engagement.

Just now, they were seated in the departure lounge at Tucson's airport.

Lawrence and Leila had decided to fly to Los Angeles so they could get settled in their suite before he had to report to the studio. This meant that Silvey was left to take care of many business matters for Leila, who had very definite ideas about how she wanted things done.

Silvey finished her notes and glanced up to see that Dan seemed to be receiving the same kinds of instructions from Lawrence.

She and Dan had hardly spoken since Lawrence had made his big announcement, but she knew he wasn't any more thrilled about this than she was. She hoped he didn't think she was responsible for it. There was no reason he should, but she was still stung by his accusation that she had encouraged Lawrence and Leila to marry.

Silvey couldn't help wondering what had made him the way he was. Lawrence's many marriages had surely affected him, even Dan admitted that. He seemed compelled to uncover hidden motives for everything. However, he probably hadn't achieved his success in the academic world or in the publishing world by being a pushover.

His very depth and complexity was what drew her to him and warned her away. She had known him less than a week, but could barely remember what her life had been like before he'd consumed so much of her thoughts.

Silvey was concentrating so hard on Dan that she looked up and blinked in surprise when Leila said, "Don't forget, you promised to help the Warriors. Desert Haven Rest Home *still* hasn't been shut down despite the evidence we sent to the state licensing board about the dirty conditions there. Also, you'll have to keep an eye on what's happening on Branaman Mountain."

Silvey's gaze flew to Dan, who had paused in his conversation with his father and glanced around sharply. His eyes narrowed on her and Leila.

"Did you hear me, honey?" Leila asked, looking up. "It may mean filing a petition to keep people out of there. I didn't have time to look into it as closely as I wanted, but I know at least one group is trying to get permission to excavate there. It seems to me they could find out if anyone objects to having their ancestors exhumed before they start something like this. You might be able to block them with an environmental impact study."

Silvey knew who wanted to excavate, but she couldn't spoil Leila's happiness by revealing it. She felt as if something was twisting inside her, but she answered in a flat voice, "Yes, Grandma. I heard you. I'll take care of it."

Dan straightened and with one sweeping, cool glance, turned back to his father.

Silvey dragged her attention back to Leila, telling herself she couldn't give up her principles because his touch had singed her all the way through to her bones. She couldn't.

"...And don't forget to let me know if you get that promotion," she heard Lawrence saying.

Silvey looked up. "What promotion is that?"

The older man turned with a smile full of pride. "They're about to make Dan head of archaeology at his college. He's got lots of great ideas. Wants to start a museum of Southwestern Indian artifacts there."

"I don't know yet if I'll get it, Dad. The board is considering other people," Dan said mildly, but Silvey saw a sharp gleam in his eye.

Beside her she heard a faint gasp and looked over to see that Leila had caught on to the implications of what Lawrence had just said.

"I thought you were an anthropologist," Leila whispered in a faint voice.

Dan inclined his head. "I am, but I also have expertise in archaeology."

She turned a stricken face to Silvey, who gazed back and gave a small shrug. A moment of resentment flared in her. Silvey didn't know how the truth of Dan's occupation had escaped Leila, but now she was left to pick up the pieces.

*   *   *

The two of them spoke very little as they walked through the terminal and into the warm summer night after seeing Lawrence and Leila off.

Dan stood beside his car as she unlocked hers, regarding her with brooding eyes.

It was late. The parking lot lights cast a pool of brightness over them. A fresh breeze, cooler than anything they had felt all day, was blowing from the east.

"I want to know what you intend to do," he said, jingling his keys impatiently in his hand.

She looked up in surprise. "About what?"

"Branaman Mountain," he snapped, coming to stand directly in front of her.

She shook her head. "I don't know yet."

His lips pulled together and his lean face took on a pinched look. "You seemed pretty adamant about your ideas the other day in my office."

That was true. But she hadn't known him quite so well then. It was easy to condemn the work or beliefs of someone she didn't know, but quite different when she had spent a little time with him, danced with him, spent hours thinking about him, not to mention having seen her grandmother become engaged to his father.

When she didn't answer, he went on. "The best thing you can do is stay out of my way."

Silvey stared at him. "Excuse me?"

"Keep your half-baked ideals to yourself. Despite what you and your grandmother think, I'm interested in preserving history, not destroying it."

"And interested in being head of your department," she shot back, incensed. "You want to make yourself look good. It's all political nonsense.''

Anger flared into his eyes, but he kept his voice under tight control. "I don't have to answer to you or defend myself. You've already got your mind made up." He jerked his chin up arrogantly. "Keep in mind, though, that there's another reason for you to do as I ask."

Silvey clapped her hands onto her hips. "Oh, really? And what could that possibly be?"

"You want that loan, don't you?"

The hot words she'd been about to say trembled on her tongue, but she forced them back. She had done as Dan had told her, withdrawing the money Lawrence had given her and returning it to him.

"Oh," she said, with a sigh. "I forgot."

"I thought maybe you had." His look was mocking. "It's time for the two of us to come to an understanding."

"What kind of understanding?"

"I'll give you what you want if you'll give me what I want."

Her fists clenched at her sides, but Silvey managed to keep her voice steady. "In other words, I get the loan if I drop my opposition to this Branaman Mountain excavation you're planning."

"That about sums it up."

"That's blackmail."

"It's business."

He looked so sure of himself that she wanted to wrap her hands around him and shake him until his teeth rattled. He had her trapped and they both knew it.

"As I see it, what we have here is a failure to communicate."

"No," she said evenly. "What we have here is a control freak gone wild."

He ignored that stinging remark. "My father thinks it's a great idea for me to loan you what you need to buy the yogurt shop. If Lawrence is happy, Leila is happy, are you beginning to get my drift?"

"That isn't fair. You're using my love for my grandmother...."

"Just as you used my love for my father when you came to my office the other day."

Darn him! He had an answer for everything. To keep herself from saying something she would regret, Silvey took a deep breath and expelled it slowly.

"All right, what exactly is it you want me to do?"

"First of all, you're going to get me that report I asked for."

"Of course. I already agreed to that, didn't I?"

He ignored that. "Also, I've got to see your books, see how the business is going. If it looks successful, I'll have my attorney draw up the appropriate papers for the loan."

"That sounds reasonable," she admitted, but reluctance dragged at her voice.

"Don't knock me over with your enthusiasm," he said dryly.

"When do you want to see the books?"

"Tomorrow will do. I'll come by the shop in the afternoon." He walked back to his car and opened the door. Propping his foot on the door frame, he leaned his forearm on the top of the door and looked at her. "Will that suit you?"

She could give him a very vivid description of what would suit her, but instead, she nodded curtly. Before he could duck into his car, she said, "What about the excavation? What you're doing isn't right."

"Nothing's going to happen for a few days, Silvey, because I don't have the permit yet. I'll let you know when I decide."

Her deep brown eyes sparked with anger. "Oh, that's big of you."

"Don't get in a snit about this. You'll see that it's best. Maybe when I get the permit, I'll take you along. If you see the actual work we're going to do, you'll drop your opposition."

"I don't think so," she answered tightly, but he merely gave her a farewell salute and waited politely for her to precede him out of the parking lot.

Silvey slipped into her own car. She'd been too independent for too long to give up easily on something this important. It was frustrating having her hands tied like this. She had the disconcerting feeling that he was in control of her past as well as her future.

In spite of her mixed feelings about Dan, when she arrived at work the next day she put one of her employees in charge and she spent the time in the tiny office area at the back making sure that the shop's books were in order. She knew they were. Because she had no natural inclination for book-keeping she had to be extra careful with all of her entries when she put information into the computer. Besides, Walter checked her printouts regularly. However, she went back over each entry to make sure there were no mistakes that Dan could catch.

As she worked, she thought about how surprised her parents would be if they could see how meticulously she was running this business. She had been an indifferent student, getting by with average grades because her thoughts and time had been consumed with her gymnastics and acrobatic classes, and with her plans for a circus career.

Funny how having that career cut short, and discovering that she wasn't cut out for the traveling life, had focused her interest in business. She'd found that the old saying was true. The things we're forced to do often become the things we want to do.

The shop was important to her, though. She truly enjoyed the challenge. Her desire to own The Yogurt Gallery grew with each passing day. She was determined to do so, even if it meant accepting a loan from someone who didn't seem to approve of, or even like her, very much.

Silvey stifled a yawn as she bent over the desk and ran her pencil down the columns of numbers. She hadn't slept much in the past few nights, too keyed up over her grandmother's departure, and her confrontation with Dan, to relax. Instead, she had called her parents, waking them from a sound sleep and shocking them with the news of Leila's engagement. It had taken her half an hour to answer all their questions and calm them down. Her dad was determined to fly to California as soon as possible to meet the man who intended to marry his mother.

Silvey gave her head a slight shake. She still couldn't believe it herself.

She was just finishing up with the books when her employee called from the front that someone wanted to see her.

Nervously, Silvey jumped to her feet, smoothed her hair and grabbed her purse to fumble for her lipstick. She swiped some quickly across her lips, then looked dubiously down at the loose denim dress she had worn to work. The idea had been to be as cool and comfortable as possible, but now she wondered if she shouldn't have worn something more businesslike. She had a nice summer suit in a lightweight cotton and a pair of bone-colored heels that were...

Oh, good heavens, what was she thinking? It was a sign of how much Dan Wisdom unnerved her that she was even thinking crazy thoughts of summer suits and two-inch heeled pumps. She tossed her lipstick back into her bag and locked it in her desk, then spun around and went to greet Dan with a cool smile.

However, it wasn't Dan who turned and gave her a frankly appreciative look when she entered the front of the shop, but John Ramos.

Surprised, she stopped in the doorway and gave him an uncertain smile, which he took for a much warmer greeting than she had intended.

He strolled forward and leaned on the counter. "Hi, Silvey. Thought I'd come down and see what kind of operation you're running here." He glanced around as he tucked his sunglasses into the neck of the Phoenix Suns T-shirt he wore with faded jeans. "I'm surprised you're in the retail business. With your acrobatic talent, I'd think you'd be able to get a job performing just about anywhere."

"I . . . I suppose I could have."

"I should have done what you did," he said. "Gone on the road instead of tying myself down to college, debts, wives, and more debts."

She hated listening to him poor-mouth, so she said, "We all make choices that we sometimes regret."

"Do you regret leaving the entertainment business?"

"Not anymore. I was tired of the traveling," she said, walking out from behind the counter to lead him out of the path of the paying customers. She couldn't imagine why he was here. She'd always liked John, but beyond their high school gymnastic competitions, they'd had little in common. "And I'm buying this shop. I've got big plans for it."

He gave her an indulgent smile, but she refused to let him make her feel inferior. Instead, she smiled back and said, "Can I get you something? Strawberry cheesecake swirl is the frozen yogurt flavor of the day. Maybe with some chocolate sprinkles on top?"

He shook his head. "No, thanks, I didn't stop in for a snack. I came to take you up on your offer."

"My offer?" Frowning, she glanced at him, then found her attention caught by the bell over the door which jingled as someone came in.

It was Dan, whose swift gaze riveted on her immediately, then darted to John. A flash of sardonic humor filled his eyes for just a second before he turned to shut the door.

She sensed John stiffen beside her and she gave him a curious look as Dan walked across to join them. The two men greeted each other and she sensed a definite coolness in their tones. Neither of them offered to shake hands, but perhaps that wasn't unexpected since they saw each other frequently at the college.

To her further surprise, the tension between them seemed to fill the shop like a living presence. Uncomfortably, Silvey wondered why they disliked each other so.

When neither of them spoke, Silvey's glance darted from one to the other and she burst into nervous speech. "Hello, Dan. John just stopped by for..." She stared at him. "Why *did* you stop by?"

He spoke to Silvey, but his eyes were on Dan. "To see if you'd like to come with me to a faculty barbecue at Dr. Varga's home. He's president of Sonora College, you know."

"No, uh, I didn't know." She glanced at Dan, who was regarding John with cool speculation. "It sounds..." Her words trailed off as she tried to decipher what Dan was thinking, then could have kicked herself for even caring.

"Now, don't say you won't go with me," John wheedled. "You said I could call you."

"Well, yes, of course, but this is a little unexpected."

"Why, Silvey? You knew I always had a thing for you."

Dan made a sound in his throat that sounded suspiciously like a cross between a laugh and a snort of derision.

John turned to look at him. "What about you, Wisdom? Will you be going?"

"Not likely. I'm not much of a schmoozer."

"Not worried about that promotion, then?"

Silvey could see that John's interest was more than idle curiosity, but she couldn't quite put her finger on the underlying tone of his voice.

Dan seemed to have no such problem. He gave John a quelling look, but he spoke in a matter-of-fact tone when he said, "If I'm promoted to head of the archaeology department, it'll be because of my work, my published papers, and my knowledge, not my attendance at faculty barbecues. I'm not bucking for anyone else's job, and I don't need to impress anyone."

Silvey watched in astonishment as a tide of red washed into John's face. Was his plan to move in on someone else's job? She suspected it was, but she still felt sorry for him because she knew how hard it was to win any kind of verbal contest with Dan. She rushed to smooth things over. "John, I'll be happy to attend with you. When is it and what shall I wear?"

She would have had to be blind to miss the disapproval in Dan's face and the flash of triumph in John's eyes as he looked first at Dan, then back to her as he gave her the information she needed.

Silvey was glad to see John out the door a few minutes later, but she turned back to Dan with a sinking heart. She really didn't want to go out with John, not to a faculty barbecue, or anywhere else. It irritated her that Dan's disapproving presence had made her feel coerced into accepting John's invitation. The truth was that she had foolishly gotten herself into this, though. She would brazen it out.

"Wasn't that nice of him to drop by?" she asked brightly.

Dan lifted a sandy brown eyebrow at her. "Oh, yes. I've noticed that John Ramos is awash in kindness."

"We're old friends," she said archly as she signaled for him to follow her into the tiny office.

"Looks to me like he's anxious to be more than old friends. In fact, he probably doesn't want to be friends at all."

"I'm sure you're wrong."

"No, I think he's got you all picked out for wife number three."

"Oh, don't be ridiculous."

Angrily, she waved toward a chair that was wedged in between the desk and the wall, then dropped into her own chair behind the desk. When he sat down, she began arranging the books, computer printouts, and receipts for him to see.

He didn't even glance at them. Instead, he studied her until she looked up and self-consciously began toying with the collar of her dress.

"What is it?" she finally asked.

"I think that in the absence of your grandmother and your parents, I should look out for you."

Her eyes sprang wide in surprise. "Look *out* for me?"

He nodded. "To make sure you don't get yourself into any trouble with a guy like John Ramos."

"John is all right. I told you, I've known him since high school."

"He's not some pimply faced kid any longer. He's a man with a man's problems, and he's not someone you should trust."

With an effort, Silvey kept her voice under control as she said, "I don't need you to tell me who I can trust."

He held up his hands, but it wasn't a sign of surrender. "Just venturing an opinion." He paused. "I hope you enjoy the barbecue."

"I'm sure I will." She gave him a smile that would have melted an iceberg.

"It's a good thing you're an acrobat."

She knew he was trying to get a rise out of her, but she couldn't help taking the bait. "Why is that?"

"Because you might need to vault over a wall to get away from him."

"I can take care of myself," she said tightly. "Now, did you want to look at these books, or not?"

With a look that told her the subject was changing only because he allowed it, Dan pulled the neat ledgers toward him and began poring over the facts and figures.

What had she been thinking? Silvey looked around the huge flagstone patio of the Varga home and tried to recall why she had agreed to this. This was not her kind of gathering. These people were all older than she was and, nice though they appeared to be, she could find little in common with them.

The setting was beautiful; a spacious home in the foothills of the Santa Catalina mountains, whose flagstone patio looked out over the city of Tucson.

At this time of the evening, the smog was obscured and only the lights could be seen, stretching far into the distance. The grounds were landscaped with desert plants and graveled paths. Delicate limbs of desert willows danced and swayed in the breeze that drifted up from the valley. A misting system had been attached to the patio roof, sending a cooling superfine spray of water into the air.

Silvey glanced around once more at the crowd. She had never regretted not going to college. She had never believed that higher education was for her, but now she wished she'd had a few classes in philosophy or logic to keep up with the dear little man who was waving his drink around and spouting about the importance of some obscure German thinker.

"Never received the kind of recognition he deserved, you know," her companion said.

"Really, Professor Roarke?" she asked, stifling a smile at his sincerity. "That's too bad. Why was that, I wonder?"

Her halfhearted encouragement was all the little professor needed to be off and running again.

Silvey couldn't help feeling piqued at John for having dumped her here while he made the rounds of the party guests. She had known he was self-serving, but she hadn't expected him to be so downright rude. He had left her to her own devices while he "schmoozed," as Dan had called it. She watched him as he left one group and moved to another and couldn't help wondering how many people recognized his basic insincerity.

Chagrined at her uncharitable thoughts, she swept her hair back from her neck and thought wistfully of a swim in the pool at the other side of the patio. It looked as if it was strictly for show, rarely used by Dr. and Mrs. Varga, who seemed to be sincere, quiet people comfortably settled into middle age. She doubted that they swam laps, but she might be wrong.

She'd been wrong about several things lately, especially about accepting this date with John. She gave Professor Roarke another smile, but her eyes wandered to where John was currently buttonholing two women whose tie-dyed clothing and strings of beads look as though they were caught in a time warp from the sixties. Since he had spent very little time with her, it was more than obvious that he hadn't brought her along as a real date, so she had to wonder why he *had* brought her along. She had assumed it was to renew an old acquaintance, but again, she'd been wrong.

She remembered the tension between him and Dan. Was it possible that John was only pursuing her because he thought Dan was interested in her? Little did he know that Dan's only interest was in "looking out for her."

Her gaze drifted to the doorway leading from the house and she froze. For some unexplained reason, a tide of heat washed through her body and reddened her face when she saw Dan Wisdom standing there.

He was dressed casually in khaki trousers and a striped shirt whose sleeves were rolled up over his forearms. He looked at ease and comfortable, unlike John, who had worn overpriced designer slacks, a silk shirt and tie to this event. As irritating as she often found Dan to be, she had to admit that was one thing she liked about him. He was sure of himself. He was a real man whereas John was just playing at being one.

Surprised at her own insight, Silvey gave a fleeting thought to the memory of how he'd looked in evening dress and sighed mentally. If he wasn't so darned good-looking and appealing, she'd have a much easier time keeping her mind off him.

Silvey bit her lip in consternation. Who was she trying to fool? His looks didn't have as much to do with her growing attraction to him as his enigmatic personality.

He intrigued her as well as irritated her.

Recalling that he'd told her he avoided such events as this, she wondered why he had come.

His sharp eyes were searching the area intently and when they met hers, she gave an involuntary shiver. As soon as he saw her, he started her way.

CHAPTER SIX

"HELLO, Silvey," Dan said, breaking right into what Professor Roarke had been saying, but the older man didn't seem to mind. He smiled when Dan greeted him, but his pleasure quickly turned to a frown when Dan added, "You know, George, I think Randall Fine disagrees with you on that point you were just making about Schwartz's theories."

"Not really!" Professor Roarke turned to seek out his adversary with the directness of a bloodhound on the scent. "Where is he?"

"I just saw him over by that tray of canapés. If you hurry, you can catch him and straighten him out."

"You're right," the professor declared. Before he turned away, he grabbed Silvey's hand and pumped it enthusiastically as he said, "Thank you for a stimulating conversation, Miss Carlton. Perhaps I'll see you later." He bustled away.

Silvey pursed her lips and gave Dan an ironic look. "That was really low, Dr. Wisdom."

Dan answered with a sly grin. "No, it isn't. Randall does disagree with him. The two of them disagree about everything under the sun. They love to argue. In fact, they *live* to argue." He tilted his head. "He seems to have enjoyed his conversation with you."

Shrugging, Silvey took a sip of her soft drink. "I can't imagine why. I hardly said a word."

"Few people do when George is around." Dan's face grew speculative as he glanced across the patio to where John was talking to Dr. Varga. "Looks like you didn't need my warning about vaulting over a wall to get away from him."

"No," she said slowly, reminding herself to keep a lid on her temper. "I didn't."

"Did your boyfriend leave you to your own devices?"

Silvey bit back the automatic denial that John was her boyfriend. Instead, she lifted her chin and said, "He does seem to have a great many people to talk to."

"Sure he does. He's campaigning for my job."

"You mean, if you get the promotion to head of the department?"

"That's right."

Silvey thought that in that case, John should be a little more deferential to Dan, but he probably knew, as she did, that Dan would scorn him. She was quiet for a minute before she asked, "Didn't I hear you say you usually avoid this kind of get-together?"

Dan feigned innocence. "Who me?"

"In fact, I heard you say that just yesterday."

"Nah," he said, with a quick shake of his head. "Must have been some other guy you were talking to. Hey, looks like they're going to serve the food. Let's go."

Dan took her arm and propelled her toward the fully loaded buffet table, sweeping her past John, who held out his hand as if to stop them.

"Wait, Silvey...."

"Excuse us," Dan said, neatly sidestepping and taking Silvey with him. "Your date is hungry."

"Then I'll take care of her," John said, icily polite.

Dan gave him a dismissive look. "Like you have all evening? I don't think so."

John squawked a protest, but when several people turned to see what was going on, his face reddened and he subsided. Silvey looked over her shoulder in time to see him give Dan a black look.

When they were in line, she pulled her arm pointedly from Dan's grasp and whispered fiercely, "What is it with you two, anyway? I'm not some kind of pull toy to be fought over by two little boys."

Dan's glance was swift. "No, you're a woman who accepts a date with a man she hasn't seen in years for the purpose of what?" He shrugged. "Having a good time? Playing us off against each other?"

Appalled by the unfairness of that accusation, Silvey stared at him while a haze of anger seemed to block out everything in her field of vision. It took her several seconds to get her voice back and when she spoke, she made sure it was low enough for only him to hear. "I won't even justify that with a denial. You know perfectly well I didn't do any such thing. I don't know why you have such a low opinion of me or why you dislike me, my grandmother, women in general, but it seems to be your problem. Not mine."

Turning, she grabbed a plate and made her way down the buffet table, loading up with more food than she normally ate in a full day. The serving spoons shook in her hand. The salad tongs trembled as she placed a small mound of salad on her plate, sending a cherry tomato rolling and bouncing away across the tabletop.

While she was doing all this, she could feel Dan just behind her shoulder. She didn't know if he wanted to speak to her, and she was hurt and angry enough not to care. In fact, she was tempted to tell him to forget about the loan altogether.

She could give up her dream of owning the shop. These push-me, pull-you confrontations with Dan were getting to be too much for her. It wasn't worth the emotional pain she was experiencing with this man.

Silvey thought about her grandmother, but decided that she could explain things to Leila, tell her grandmother that she and Dan simply couldn't get along. If Lawrence offered once again to loan her the money, she would refuse. Getting involved with the Wisdom men in any way was more than she could stand.

Ignoring Dan, she looked for a place to eat by herself. John was far back in the line and wouldn't be joining her for a while—if he ever did. She walked swiftly away from Dan and found a single chair by a small table. Jerking the chair forward, she sat, then stared helplessly at the mountain of food on her plate, then pushed it away. She didn't want all of this. She didn't want any of it.

She sensed someone standing behind her, but knowing it was Dan, she didn't glance up until she heard the scrape of another chair being dragged over to join her. Then her gaze shot up, her eyes full of fire.

Before she could speak, Dan said, "I'm sorry."

The furious words she'd been forming slipped away before they could be spoken and she blinked at him. His eyes didn't leave her face as he pulled his chair around with one hand and sat down, positioning his plate across from hers. He'd placed only a few items on it and at any other time, Silvey would have laughed at the incongruous pair they made.

"I apologize for acting like a bastard," he said. His tone was sincere, but his face was shuttered.

She hated that he was so hard to read—and she was so easy. "Why did you?" she demanded. She picked up her fork, speared a bite of lettuce, then set it down again. "I never know where I am with you," she complained.

"And you want to?"

Frustrated, Silvey used both hands to shove her golden brown hair away from her face, then placed them on the tabletop and leaned forward. Soft curls immediately sprang forward to bounce around her unhappy face. "Like it or not, we are linked together, and…and that's hard for me to…take." She stopped, took a breath, and looked into the darkness beyond the patio lights, opening her eyes wide and willing away unwelcome tears. Her eyes glittered when she looked back at him.

His gaze touched on her face and his lips pinched together. "Silvey," he began, but she cut him off.

"Two weeks ago, I didn't even know you existed. Now my grandmother is engaged to your father, you're providing the loan for me to buy my shop...." And she spent far too much time thinking about him. She took a shuddering breath and went on. "I've tried to watch what I've said around you. I'm used to saying what I think and...well, I'm going to say it now."

"Go ahead," he said, but she didn't need his permission. She had a head of steam going now and he couldn't have stopped her if he'd tried.

"You don't really know me. I mean, how could you? We've just met and the circumstances haven't exactly been ordinary, and yet you always seem to think the worst of me. As I said before, it's not my problem. It's your problem."

Defiantly, she stared at him, her chest heaving with quick breaths and lingering anger.

Of course he didn't react in the way she might have expected—not that she knew what she did expect.

His face softened and his mouth lifted in a self-mocking smile. "I guess you do know me after all."

She blinked at him. "What?"

Instead of answering, he asked, "Are you really hungry?"

"What? Oh, no." She gave up any pretense of eating and pushed the plate aside.

"Then let's get out of here," he suggested. "I'll tell John you've got a headache and I'm taking you home."

Silvey would have protested, but he was already several yards away. The conversation between the two men was short, and from what she could see, fiercely polite. She should have felt bad about leaving John, but he'd invited her, then left her alone all evening. As angry as she was at Dan, she couldn't imagine him doing such a thing.

John accompanied Dan back to her. Stiffly, he wished her good-night, saying he hoped she felt better soon. With a brittle smile, she nodded and turned away, but she felt his angry gaze burning between her shoulder blades as she went.

Dan's hand rode firmly at the small of her back, ushering her along. He helped her negotiate her way through the crowd, thank the solicitous Vargas, and assure them she would be perfectly all right. In no time, Dan had her outside and into his car. He started the motor and drove slowly down the mountainside while she stared straight ahead and tried to sort through the emotions that were battering her.

Anger was still uppermost, but she also felt a keen disappointment. It hurt that Dan thought so little of her and it hurt even more that she didn't know why. When she began to calm down a little, she stole a quick glance at him. His face was grim in the pale golden glow of the dashboard lights. His jaw was set.

He was such an enigma, she felt she would never know him. She turned away and crossed her arms beneath her breasts, grasping her elbows. At this moment, she wasn't sure she wanted to. She couldn't help comparing him to Lawrence, who seemed so open and easy to read. The comparison might not be fair, though. There were depths and layers to Dan's personality that she hadn't detected in his father. In many ways he was a man apart. She would never know him unless he allowed her to.

Dan slowed the car, then eased onto a wide pullout area that overlooked the city. They were several hundred feet below the Varga home, but the view was still spectacular. Silvey wanted to ask why they'd stopped, but she was determined that he would speak first.

Dan switched off the motor and sat with his hands gripping the wheel. Finally, he let them slip down to lie loosely on his thighs.

After several tense moments, he said, "Silvey, the Wisdom men aren't a good bet for a long-term relationship."

She turned in her seat to stare at him. "Are you talking about Lawrence, or about yourself?"

"Both," he answered, looking out into the night.

Silvey's hands clenched in her lap, but she kept her tone even. "Dan, do you plan to try and break up Lawrence and Leila's engagement?"

"Not actively. But if it shatters of its own accord, the Wisdom men will be running true to form."

"That's a very cynical view."

"But realistic."

The certainty in his voice made her feel sick with disappointment. Again, she wondered what had made him like this. She said, "It'll be different for Lawrence with Grandma. You'll see."

Dan didn't argue. "Then I guess I'm talking about myself."

"Are you saying there have been a succession of women in your life, too?"

Dan turned to her then, and she thought she heard a hint of a smile in his voice. "Do I look like the type of man who kisses and tells?"

On a sigh of frustration, she said, "How would I know, Dan? As I said, in spite of the time we've spent together, I hardly know you."

He accepted that in a brooding silence that lasted several seconds before he went on. "I'm talking about my dad's women. My stepmothers. The ones who married him and stayed for a few months or a few years, at best. Hell, Silvey," he said, in disgust. "There have been so many women pass through our lives, I never knew which ones to trust because I never knew which ones would be staying around."

In his voice she didn't hear a little boy's whine, but the resignation of a man who had come to terms with what had happened to him.

"What about your mother?"

"I don't remember her. Dad's never talked about their marriage very much except to say that he was just too hard to live with. There were always too many people around. Friends, hangers on, acquaintances wanting a handout. They never had a real family life. Knowing him now, as an adult, I can look at him and see that he was too much like a shooting star or a comet she couldn't hang on to."

"What was she like?"

"I only have secondhand information to go by. She was the script girl on one of Dad's movies. Young and drop-dead gorgeous from what I hear. She was desperate to be an actress, but she had no talent, so somebody had given her the job on the set. Dad says that for all her glamorous beauty, she was a small-town Missouri girl at heart. Probably should have stayed there, married and raised a couple of kids instead of seeking her fortune in Hollywood." Dan paused before adding, "She died when I was two."

"Oh, Dan," Silvey said in soft dismay as she imagined what it would have been like growing up without her mother in a household where the cast of characters was always changing. "That's terrible."

Dan shrugged. "It's in the past now."

"But the past affects the present."

"Only if we let it," Dan said grimly.

Silvey turned away, shaking her head. "Cynicism, again."

"I told you, I'm a realist. I hope things work out for Dad and Leila. She's not like anyone else he's ever married."

Silvey frowned at the strangeness of that phrase.

"When he met my mother," Dan continued, "Dad was twenty years older than she was, already married, but he had to have her." Dan made a low, snorting sound, but Silvey heard no bitterness in his voice. "It might have been better if Dad had been capable of unfaithfulness."

She gave a small laugh of disbelief. "Dan, what a thing to say."

"I mean, he was too much of a gentleman to begin an affair with another woman while he was still married, so he divorced one wife before taking up with the next one. He always made sure his ex-wives had plenty of money. One of them told me that he made a better ex-husband than a husband. My mother only lasted a couple of years. She left when I was a few months old and died of pneumonia two years later."

Silvey grimaced. Her anger at him had dissipated and she couldn't help laying a comforting hand over his. "I'm sorry, Dan."

"It was a long time ago, and I don't brood over it. I know it's my choice to be like my dad or not."

"I beg your pardon?"

Dan's shoulders shifted restlessly against the seat back. "I'm trying to explain why I've acted like a bastard."

Silvey sighed helplessly. "You must be better at explaining in print than you are in person because I still don't understand."

"Dad always seemed to fall for the next pretty girl to come along."

"And?"

"Hell, I didn't expect it to happen to me."

"What do you mean?"

"I mean, I've avoided entanglements. I've known a lot of women. I've been with many women, but they all knew the score, knew that I wasn't going to fall in love with them."

"And you never did?"

"I never let myself."

"And now?"

"Hell, I don't know," he sighed. "I never expected to go rushing out to rescue my dad from another gold digger only to meet a mature lady whose only interest is Dad's welfare, and a girl who dances with mops."

Silvey blinked, then began to smile. Her smile grew into a grin. "Are you saying in your own endearingly convoluted way that you've fallen for me?"

He didn't answer directly, but in a tone of self-disgust he said, "I was jealous that you'd gone to that damned barbecue with Ramos."

Her mouth dropped open in a surprised *O*. "Well, I... I'm stunned."

"Not half as stunned as I am. I'd never planned to let a woman get that kind of hold over me."

All her other emotions gave way before a flood of tenderness. "We can't always plan what happens to us, Dan."

His hand flexed beneath hers, then turned over to entwine with her fingers. "Don't I know it."

The irony in his voice might have made her smile if his tone hadn't been heavily resigned. She looked into his eyes, trying to read his expression, but his face, and his thoughts, were in shadow. The idea of having any kind of power over him, much less an emotional power, rocked her back on her heels.

He leaned forward and lifted his hand to cup her jaw, firmly, but gently holding her in place. Silvey started in surprise, but he made a quiet, soothing sound. She could see his eyes now. They were darkly intent. In spite of the evening's warmth, shivers swept over her in a tide. Her jaw trembled beneath his touch.

"I've concentrated on my career. That's been enough."

"Has it? Is that why you've got two successful careers? To fill up your time?"

"Partly."

Silvey was saddened for him. She had known from the minute they met that he was a man of determination and purpose. Too bad he used it to close himself off from so much of life.

"I've avoided involvement my whole adult life," he added.

"Have you? That's too bad." Her eyes were begging to drift shut so she could concentrate on his touch, his nearness.

"I've seen for myself that involvement brings all kinds of hazards—messy emotional situations that are usually only solved with a checkbook." The tip of his finger ran over the soft outer shell of her ear. "It's a void in my life, but it's one I've come to live with."

"Oh, Dan," she said sadly, but her voice hiccuped on a sound of desire.

Silvey whimpered as heat began to swirl through her. She had to fight the sensual fog he was creating with his touch to focus on what he was saying. "You're not being fair, Dan Wisdom."

"Sure I am. I'm letting you know exactly where I stand." Dan leaned close to her and they were inches away from each other when he said, "I have to tell you, Silvey, I still don't intend to let a woman have that kind of power over me."

"Then what are you doing?" she whispered unsteadily.

"Damned if I know." Dan slipped his fingers into her hair, loosening a wave that fell down over his forearm.

Silvey knew what was coming, but it was still a shock when his mouth closed over hers. The kiss was long and slow, exploring and questioning.

Their position was awkward—side by side, turned at an uncomfortable angle toward each other, but neither of them seemed to notice.

Silvey was too enthralled by his taste and his touch, too shocked by the depth of feeling that swept through her when his lips pressed against hers, drew away while he stared at her, then returned in a fresh rush of desire.

Her hand stole up to his arm, running over the sharp ridge of his elbow, then across his biceps, which felt hard and smooth beneath her palm, to his shoulder, then around his neck.

She couldn't have said how long the kiss lasted because she was too involved in prolonging it. She wanted to draw from him the answer to every question she'd had about him since the moment they met.

It would have been impossible for her to say what a cynic tasted or felt like, but surely it wasn't this wonderful warmth, this sweet, heady rush of desire that was beginning to flame through her.

She should have known it would be like this, she thought hazily. When she had danced with him, she had suspected these depths of feeling. She just hadn't suspected that the depths would close over her head so quickly, leaving her inseparably tied to him, swamped in her own emotions.

Finally, Dan pulled his mouth from hers, slipped his lips over her cheek, and kissed her jaw.

She shivered and in a shaky voice, said, "Dan, I don't know what you're thinking, but to me, this doesn't feel like noninvolvement."

Dan went instantly still. His lips were against her cheek. She felt a flutter on her skin, and knew it was his eyelashes. He was probably squeezing his eyes tight against the emotions inside him. She wished she knew what they were.

His hands lifted to her shoulders and he set her firmly but gently away from him. "You're right. Where you're concerned, I seem to say one thing and do another."

Silvey stared at him in dismay, but couldn't think of anything to say. The excitement of his touch was still boiling through her, even as he withdrew it. Her lips wanted further contact with his mouth, even as his lips apologized for touching her.

So far this evening, she had been hurt and angry. Now she felt a vast hollow of sorrow inside her. She struggled against threatening tears and took refuge in flippancy. Tossing her head, she scooted back to her own side of the seat and said, "Then I'd better go against what my mother always told me."

"What's that?"

Silvey lifted her chin. "My mom is big on pithy sayings such as 'actions speak louder than words', but in your case I'm going to have to judge you by your words and not by your actions."

He gave her a quick look. "Why is that?"

"Because you don't seem to know what you want."

"You're wrong, Silvey," he said on a soft note of scorn. "I know exactly what I want, but you're not the type of woman to give it to me—at least not yet."

Her head whipped around in the darkness as she tried to read his expression. "Do you mean an affair?"

"That's right, and it's not going to happen," he said ruthlessly. "It's best if we stay out of each other's way."

Silvey couldn't have said why that hurt. After all, he was right. She wasn't the kind of woman who indulged in affairs. She would have to be in love with a man before she slept with him, and how could she love a man who didn't love her back? Who didn't even trust such an emotion as love? Even though she felt as battered as an old soccer ball, she manufactured a proud tone in her voice. "You're right. You're giving me a loan. I'll pay it back. There's nothing but business between us."

Dan's hands curled slowly around the steering wheel. "Silvey, you're fooling yourself. There's far more between us than business, but we both need time to decide what that is. As I said, we need to stay out of each other's way—for a while at least." He paused, seeming to expect an answer from her, but she couldn't formulate words. Finally, he said, "I'll take you home now."

She nodded, silent with misery, unable to answer for fear that the sound of her breaking heart would echo in her voice.

Silvey didn't see Dan again for a week. The night he'd brought her home from the Vargas' party, he'd walked her to her door, said a polite good night, and strolled away. The next day, his attorney called to say that the papers for the loan from Dan were ready. As soon as she signed, the money would be hers.

Expecting to see Dan at the attorney's office, she'd dressed carefully in a pale yellow summer suit and made the journey to downtown Tucson, only to find that a secretary handled all the details. Silvey had driven away with a large check and a heavy heart, telling herself that she wasn't in love with him so her disappointment at not seeing him shouldn't have been so fierce, but she couldn't help recalling what he'd said about messy emotional situations that were solved with a checkbook. She knew he hadn't been talking about this loan, but still, she felt as if she'd been bought off.

After depositing the check, she made the arrangements with the owner and in no time, The Yogurt Gallery was hers. She closed the shop for a couple of days, and with promises of substantial bonuses, induced her employees to help her paint and wallpaper the place, and arrange the consigned artwork in eye-catching displays near the door.

While all this was going on, the activist group that Leila had left in her charge was growing increasingly restless. As much as she loved her grandmother, Silvey wished she could have found someone else to take over this group. She regretted agreeing to lead them, but she knew Leila was depending on her.

Dutifully, she called a meeting and the group that called themselves Leila's Warriors met at her house one afternoon to sit around her kitchen table, drink lemonade, eat cookies, and discuss strategy.

As soon as they sat down, Frank and Lupe Beltran, a feisty elderly couple, announced that they had finally persuaded an inspector to make an unannounced visit to the rest home whose conditions they found so distasteful.

Silvey eyed them warily as they snickered. ''Oh? How did you do that?''

''By camping in front of his office door until he agreed,'' Lupe said with a smug smile.

"I don't think he liked having two people with a cooler of soft drinks, a dozen sandwiches, and two sleeping bags cluttering up his office," Frank said.

"How narrowminded of him." Silvey grinned, imagining the scene. "Now let's just hope he makes that place clean up its act." She looked around at the group. "So? What's next?"

"The Branaman Mountain excavation," Reed Madison answered with obvious relish. He was the oldest and the most vocal of the group—verging on militant. "We've all heard the rumors that Sonora College is interested in digging there. I tried to contact the head of their archaeology department, but he just retired due to ill health. Someone he dug up probably put a curse on him." The old man cackled. "No one else there would talk to me."

Including Dr. Daniel Wisdom, no doubt, Silvey thought. She could suggest that they try to meet with him, but right now he was only a professor. If he succeeded in excavating Branaman Mountain, he would be made department head. Yet, if he did excavate, he would be going against everything she believed. And he had told her to stay out of his way where the mountain was concerned—and where he was concerned.

Silvey's heart sank when she thought about him. He had certainly carried through on his promise to give her the loan she needed. She doubted that he would ask for the money back if she interfered with his excavation. But he had also kissed her in a way that was sweet enough to melt her heart while saying he didn't want any woman to have a hold over him.

When the group stopped chortling, Reed went on. "I contacted the tribal councils of several state tribes. They agreed to send letters of protest to the state about the planned excavation."

"But they can't really speak for the Morenos. They're not part of that tribe," Silvey said.

"Exactly what does the law say about excavating burial sites?" Frank wanted to know.

"That burial grounds must remain undisturbed unless the tribe wants them moved or they're threatened by a building project. In this case, a road up to the telescope site is supposed to go in there eventually."

"That's the project we really need to stop," Reed said hotly. "Can't the road be put somewhere else?"

"Maybe," Silvey answered. "It might be possible to block that if we can stop the burial site excavation."

"I think we need to do something more," Lupe chimed in.

"Like what?" Silvey asked, although she had a feeling she knew what was coming.

"Stage a protest," she announced, looking around for approval, which the other members gave readily.

Silvey shook her head. "That's fenced government land. We can't go up there without a permit."

"Seems pretty funny to me that citizens of the United States have to have permission to go on property they own," Lupe sniffed.

"You know it's to keep vandals, squatters, and illegal hunters off." Silvey looked around at the little group. She agreed with their sentiments, but had often taken issue with their methods.

"It wouldn't do us any good to go there, anyway," Frank said. "We wouldn't get any media coverage." He cocked his head to one side, deep in thought. "It needs to be something more visible."

As they considered, Silvey recalled yet again that although Dan had told her to stay out of his way, her own belief was that she should do so. She also remembered her grandfather's pride in his Moreno heritage; the few stories he had told her of tribal lore, the sacredness of the final resting place. She took a deep breath.

"Sonora College has already asked permission to excavate up there." She immediately had the attention of the others, who looked concerned. "If we got the rest of the group together and picketed the college itself, I'll bet we could get a television news crew out."

Reed was almost licking his chops. "Yeah," he breathed. "That's a great idea."

"We're doing it legally this time, though," Silvey warned, shaking her finger at them. "We'll get a permit to assemble at the edge of the college's property. No trouble this time."

Her cohorts gave her looks of perfect innocence. "Of course, Silvey. Whatever you say."

Considering their history, she didn't feel reassured.

CHAPTER SEVEN

SONORA College was at the east end of town in an area just developing into residential and industrial parks. Tucson's building boom of the eighties had slowed in this particular area so civilization wasn't rushing in on the campus quite yet. It stood on a large tract only a mile from a major interstate highway. There was room for them to build a museum and, with easy access from the highway as well as from town, it wouldn't lack for visitors.

When Silvey arrived, few of Leila's Warriors were there so she parked across the road, rolled down her windows to let in the gritty breeze and popped the lid of a lemon-lime soda. As she sipped the cold drink, she considered the afternoon's plans.

The group would march calmly with placards denouncing the planned excavation of the Moreno burial site. When television news teams arrived, Reed Madison would read a prepared statement, then the group would disperse peacefully. Reading the statement was an honor that usually fell to Leila, but Silvey had insisted Reed do it in exchange for his promise not to make up any militaristic marching slogans for the group to shout.

Silvey took another sip of soda and surveyed the site. At least there wouldn't be any difficulty in keeping the group off the college's property since they were separated from the campus by a wide boulevard.

113

She still wished she didn't have charge of the group, but at least it wouldn't be for long. Grandma and Lawrence would be home in a few weeks and Silvey didn't think her grandmother was going to be very interested in continuing her activities with the group.

Last night she had received a giddy phone call from Leila, who was agog at her temporary home at the Beverly Hills Hotel. She couldn't say enough ecstatic things about Lawrence, who had already gone to work on the miniseries, leaving Leila to explore Hollywood when she was alone during the day. She insisted everything was just perfect and that Dan had even called and talked to his father for a long time.

Leila said she had been tempted to eavesdrop, worrying over Dan's plans for Branaman Mountain and that Silvey should withdraw her protest to the excavation. Silvey had tried to soothe her, but in truth, she was worried, too, but not about the same thing.

She was inclined to think their conversation had concerned Lawrence and Leila's coming marriage, even though she believed Dan when he said he wouldn't actively try to break them up.

Thoughts of Dan stitched a frown between Silvey's eyebrows. She had a pretty good idea what she was going to say when he found out what she was up to. He had made it clear that he would withhold the loan if she got in the way of his excavation. Now that she had the loan, she felt that she was being dishonest by going ahead with the protest, and yet, she couldn't back down. This was important, and besides, there was no telling what

Leila's Warriors might do if she wasn't around to watch over them.

Silvey gulped the rest of her soda, and glanced around to see that the members of her group had all arrived. The news team was due in fifteen minutes, which would work out fine. She didn't want the Warriors, most of whom were elderly, to be in the sun too long.

She set down her empty soda can and reached around to pull her placard from the small space behind the seat. As she did so, a flash of color caught her eye and she turned to see Dan Wisdom's car pulling up behind hers.

Silvey froze with her eyes wide and her fingers wrapped around the wooden handle of her sign. She hadn't seen him since the night he had told her he didn't want to get involved, then kissed her senseless. Remembering how she had felt in his arms, Silvey decided she could be forgiven for the way her heart leaped up and began pounding in her throat.

He jumped out of his car and strode toward her. Today he was dressed in snug jeans and a blue T-shirt and didn't look the least bit professorial. In fact, he made her mouth water. She swallowed quickly and turned around when he stopped at the passenger side of her car and stuck his head in the open window.

"What are you doing here, Silvey?" he asked as his gaze fell to her sign. " 'Let The Moreno Indians Rest In Peace,' " he quoted, then looked back at her, his eyes like blue ice chips. "Not very original."

"Actually, that's one of our milder slogans," she said, and cursed herself for the faintness in her voice.

"*Our*?"

She climbed out of the car and pointed to the assembled group. They waved to her cheerily as they began walking in circles, placards held proudly aloft.

Dan stared, then looked at her in amazement. "What did you do, raid an old folks' home?"

Silvey took a deep breath and plunged in. "This is the group Grandma was talking about when we left her and Lawrence at the airport."

"*This* is her group of activists?"

"Leila's Warriors."

Dan burst out laughing. "Oh, they look like a real threat."

She didn't like his tone. "I'll have you know, Dr. Wisdom, that they're very effective."

Dan placed his hands on his hips and looked at her in humored perplexity. "How many times per protest do you have to get out the oxygen to revive them?"

"They may be elderly, but they get the job done."

"And what job's that? Getting heatstroke? Embarrassing me? Making sure your loan is canceled?"

"You wouldn't dare." She said it, but she didn't quite believe it. Still, she lifted her chin defiantly.

Dan scowled at her. "Oh, I get it. The minute your loan went through, you thought you could ignore what I asked you to do."

Silvey's hands twisted on the wooden handle. "You didn't exactly *ask*," she hedged.

"You know what I mean." He glanced once again at the Warriors. "How did you get involved with this bunch, anyway?"

"Mostly, I just look out for them."

"Are you sure they need it?"

No, she thought, but she answered, "I promised my grandmother."

Dan placed his hands on his hips and rocked back on his heels. "You mean you keep your promises to some people, but not to others? I thought *we* had an agreement."

"No. You gave orders and I chose not to go along with them. This is important," she insisted. "What you want to do up on that mountain is wrong."

"How the hell would you know? You don't know what it is I want to do." Frustrated, he paused and paced a few steps away from her, then turned and came back. He ran a hand through his hair and pushed his glasses up on his nose. "How long do your people plan to be out here?"

She shrugged innocently. "Only until the television news crew shows up."

His eyes widened. "News...? Oh, Lord," he muttered. He watched her for a few seconds, then said, "Look, why don't you come up on the mountain with me and see what I have in mind? Maybe you can drop your complaints then."

She shaded her face with the placard and stared at him. "Come with you? To Branaman Mountain?" She couldn't keep the trace of excitement from her voice. An opportunity to visit the site before it was disturbed was more than she'd ever hoped for.

"That's right. I figure it's the only way you'll drop the protest, if you see what we really intend to do."

She glanced down so he wouldn't see the avid interest in her eyes. "Well, I guess it would be okay."

"Better take this offer. It's the only one you're going to get," he said sardonically, then made an exasperated noise. "I keep telling myself it's a mistake to have anything to do with you. I remind myself that it's pure folly, but somehow I don't listen."

Silvey tucked her tongue into her cheek. "So you told me the other night. Believe me, I haven't forgotten it."

He gave her a black look.

"Dan, are you saying I'm irresistible, or just plain irritating?"

"Flip a coin," he sighed. "It can go either way."

Her lips pressed together, Silvey gave him a disgruntled look. "Well, since you've asked me so nicely and everything, I'll be happy to go."

"Fine." He turned away. "Saturday morning. I'll pick you up at nine o'clock. Do you have any hiking boots?"

"Yes."

"Wear them and sunscreen. It'll be a long day."

No kidding. And even longer if he was this prickly and standoffish the whole time.

"I'll bring food, too," she shouted after him. "Just in case you have any ideas about starving me into submission."

"If I thought that would work, I would have tried it before now," he grumbled.

She watched him duck into his car and zip across the road to the college parking lot, then get out and stride rapidly into his office building.

This would be so much easier if she wasn't so enthralled with him, if she didn't spend so much time thinking about him. True, they had a relationship, that of creditor and debtor, but it was hardly the type she wanted.

Lowering her head in thought, she turned and scuffed rocks away with her sandals as she walked back to join the group.

She recalled what he'd told her while they'd been sitting in his car after they'd left the Vargas' barbecue. No wonder he was such an enigma, given all the upheaval he'd experienced in his young life. He felt he had to keep his emotions under control. He'd let that control slip and she wished it would happen again.

She wanted to spend time alone with him and the trip to Branaman Mountain would be the perfect opportunity. After all, he hadn't mentioned a word about anyone else coming along.

Silvey lifted her head and grinned suddenly. This trip didn't have to be exactly what he expected. It could be fun. She had already told him she would bring food. She would make it into a real picnic. Heaven knew, Dan Wisdom could use a little more fun in his life and she was just the person to provide it. True, he found her irritating, but he'd also said she was irresistible, and she knew from the way he'd kissed her that he had some feelings for her. That was something to build on.

Satisfied with that idea, she stepped lightly as she joined the group and waited for the news crew.

* * *

Saturday morning was hot and clear with no rain forecast. Silvey dressed in a yellow cotton shirt and shorts. She thought the clunky hiking boots ruined the look, but she was being careful to follow Dan's orders to the letter. By eight o'clock, she was in the kitchen, assembling the food she had prepared the night before. She had made chicken sandwiches, then sliced up carrot and celery sticks and placed them in sealed plastic bags. She'd made chocolate brownies with chocolate chips and nuts. Pinching off a bite, she let it melt in her mouth. If it was true that the way to a man's heart was through his stomach, Dan Wisdom didn't stand a chance. Placing the food in a picnic hamper, she set it by the front door, tossed a folded blanket and tablecloth over it, then hurried back to the kitchen for the cooler of bottled water and soft drinks.

She stopped, clicking her tongue in irritation when she realized she'd forgotten to buy a bag of crushed ice. A quick glance at the clock told her she could make it to the corner convenience store and back before Dan arrived. Grabbing her keys and purse, she ran out the door.

At the store, she purchased the ice and hopped back in her car only to discover that it wouldn't start. When she turned the key, she heard a faint grinding sound, then nothing. A dead battery. Silvey slumped in the seat and pressed her forehead against the steering wheel. Of all the rotten luck.

There wasn't time for her to call a tow truck and wait for it. Dan was due at her house in a few minutes, and he would have no idea where she was. She would have to walk, and hope the ice didn't melt by the time she got home.

She went back into the store and got the manager's permission to leave the car there until Monday. He helped her push it around to the side of the building and assured her it would be all right. Silvey thanked him and gave her car a disgruntled look as she picked up the dripping bag of ice, locked the car, and started home. It served her right for buying a car that was more flash than substance.

She had gone only a couple of blocks when a car pulled up alongside her and someone called out. Hot and irate, with dampness from the ice spreading over her shirt, she ignored the driver who she was sure was trying to pick her up for no good purpose. When he shouted again, she turned to give him a piece of her mind. She found herself frowning at John Ramos.

"Hey," he said. "Need a ride?"

In other circumstances, Silvey would have turned him down. She was still miffed at the way he had taken her to the Vargas' party and then left her alone. She realized now that he'd probably only invited her to irritate Dan. But she needed to get home, and he had a car that ran.

With a word of thanks, she opened the door and tumbled in. Quickly, she gave him directions to her house.

"Good thing I was going this way," he commented.

"I'm glad you happened along." Silvey looked out the window and wished he would hurry. Dan might be waiting.

"I had to go over to my ex-wife's place. New condo *I'm* paying for," he said in disgust. "Had to sign some tax papers."

Hearing his familiar lament set Silvey's teeth on edge. She felt bad that his marriages hadn't worked out, but she was beginning to understand why. What woman wanted to stay married to a man who felt sorry for himself?

"Is your freezer on the blink?" he asked, eyeing the bag of ice.

"I need enough for a cooler of soft drinks."

"Going on a picnic?"

"Yes," Silvey answered cautiously, hoping he wouldn't ask to come along.

"Anyplace special?"

She saw no harm in telling the truth. She was proud to be going somewhere with Dan, and Dan's visit to the mountain was probably common knowledge at the college. "To Branaman Mountain with Dan Wisdom. He's going to show me where they plan to excavate."

"If they get permission," John added, his dark eyes giving her a quick, sideways glance. "It'll be quite a feather in his cap if he can open up that site."

Silvey didn't like his insinuating tone. "Yes, it will." She glanced up, glad to see her own driveway up ahead, but dismayed to see an unfamiliar beige truck parked there. Dan was leaning against the side, watching their approach. His shoulders were resting on the door, his arms over his chest and his booted feet crossed at the ankles. Despite his relaxed pose, Silvey could almost feel the tension emanating from him.

John stopped the car and nodded to Dan who gave him a cool look. John's face flushed. "Some

guys get along on pure luck," he said bitterly.
"They don't have to really work for anything."

Silvey was already halfway out of the car, blurting
a quick thanks, but she stopped and stared at him.
"That's not true, John. Dan works hard. He's res-
pected in his field."

John's lip curled. "And you've got the hots for
him."

Insulted, Silvey slammed the door and stepped
back as John tromped on the gas and roared away.

Shaken by the encounter, she turned toward her
house to find Dan facing her. His feet were spread
wide apart and his hands rested on the waist of the
khaki bush shirt he wore with trousers which were
festooned with many pockets.

Because she knew he was going to say something
about John, Silvey tossed her head and gave him
a saucy look. "Have you got a pith helmet to go
with that outfit?"

His eyes never left her as he reached a hand into
the truck that had Sonora College printed on the
side. He picked up a dark brown fedora and clapped
it onto his head. Turning, he looked at her
expectantly.

Silvey gave a faint smile. "Looks like I'm going
adventuring with Indiana Jones!"

Dan reached out and took the ice from her,
holding it away so that it dripped on the sidewalk.
"I picked this hat up at Dad's old house in
California. He wore it in a movie called *The
Untamed* back in the fifties. Have you seen that
one?"

She wished she knew what he was really thinking.
It was impossible to read his expression. She hated
that they were talking all around the real problem.

Pulling her key from her purse, she started for the front door. "No. I haven't seen that movie, but the hat is definitely your style."

He didn't answer for a moment, then finally he asked quietly, "Where's your car, Silvey?"

She pushed the front door open as she gave him a challenging look over her shoulder. She recalled how he'd told her he'd felt jealous of John. At the time, she'd been amused and flattered, but now she felt sick, fearing that he thought the worst of her.

"It's not parked at John Ramos' place, if that's what you're thinking." Her voice shook and she cleared her throat, hating the way he made her feel defensive with nothing more than a lift of his eyebrows.

"It's not what I'm thinking."

With a proud tilt of her head, Silvey waved him inside and indicated the hamper beside the door. "I made us a picnic lunch, but then I realized I'd forgotten to buy ice for the cooler of soft drinks. My car stalled at the convenience store. Sounds like a dead battery. John happened along and gave me a ride."

"That was nice of him."

There hadn't been anything nice about it, and the distant expression in Dan's face was even less nice. She refused to make excuses, though. It wasn't as though he had any kind of hold over her, any more than she had one over him.

She tossed her purse onto the sofa and flounced into the kitchen. Dan followed with the bag of ice. He poured it into the cooler and she arranged the cans of soda and bottles of water. Finished, she slammed the lid and flipped the latch while Dan slowly and methodically folded the plastic bag. He looked around for a trash can.

Silvey reached for the bag, but he held on to it until she looked up at him.

Prickly and defensive, her gaze darted up to meet his. A hint of a smile edged his mouth.

"Good morning, Silvanna," he said formally.

Some of Silvey's tension began to relax. "Good morning, Daniel."

He took the plastic bag from her lax grip and tossed it into the sink. Then his fingers moved up to her wrist. He lifted her hand and placed it on his shoulder where it lay as limp with surprise as the rest of her. She blinked slowly as his hands moved around behind her. He drew her forward until she was pressed up against him. Delicious excitement replaced her surprise, spiraling through her in waves.

"What say we start this day out on the right note?" Dan's voice was low and gruff with some emotion that she hoped was the same desire she was feeling.

She had to swallow before she spoke. "What note would that be?"

He bent his head and kissed her forehead. "Oh, just a little friendliness."

Oh, Lord, he smelled wonderful. She unabashedly buried her nose in the V-opening of his shirt. "You think we can be friends?"

"That depends." His lips feathered over her temple.

She lifted her face so they would touch her cheek. She wanted to turn her lips up to meet his, but a sudden shyness held her back. "Depends on what?"

"On how much you want it."

His nearness was fogging her mind. "Oh, I want it," she sighed.

With a soft chuckle, Dan brought his mouth to hers. Silvey whimpered with pleasure at the contact. She went up on tiptoes and clasped her arms around his neck. She knew she should have resisted more. It seemed he could so easily bend her to his will, but she didn't protest.

Finally, he pulled away and looked down at her, his eyes deep blue with amusement. "I'd say that on the friendliness factor that kiss rates a ten."

Silvey drew in a shaky breath and touched her tongue to her lips. They were flushed and swollen and she loved the feeling. She released the breath in a rush and asked, "Care to try for a twenty?"

Dan laughed and released her. "If we do, we'll never get on the road."

Keenly disappointed, but wanting to hide it, Silvey gave him a sassy look. "And we don't want anything to hold us up, do we? After all, you've got to convince me you need to excavate that mountain, and I've got to convince you that you don't."

Dan gave her one of his steady looks as he picked up the cooler. "Let's go, then. We'll stop on the way back into town, and buy a battery for your car. I can install it."

Pleased, she smiled at him as she locked the door and thought about how generous he was with his time and energy. Her dream was that he could be as generous with his love. "Thanks, Dan. I would appreciate that."

Within a few minutes they had locked the house, stowed the food in a lock box in the back of the truck and headed out of town.

Branaman Mountain was northeast of the city so they started out on Interstate 10, then switched to a state road that wound through land administered by the Bureau of Land Management. Cattle dotted the mesquite and creosote-covered hills that rolled away into the hazy distance.

The truck didn't have air-conditioning so they cranked down both windows and let the desert heat blast through. The less than ideal conditions didn't seem to bother either of them. Dan asked Silvey how the shop was coming along and she knew they'd reached a truce.

Enthusiastically, she told him of the new paint job that had brightened the place up and thanked him again for the loan.

Dan waved his hand negligently. "It's just money. I've got plenty of that."

Silvey gave him a puzzled look and settled against the seat. A few weeks ago he'd been adamant that she and her grandmother weren't going to get their hands on his father's money. Now it didn't seem important to him. She understood now that the issue had never been the actual cash, but the threat to his father's emotional and financial stability.

Dan himself was easygoing about money. His financial situation was obviously secure, as were his emotions—at least the ones he let her see. It was his hidden emotions that intrigued her, his hidden desires and needs.

She knew what he would like to have from her— an affair, but he wouldn't ask it of her. Because of that, or maybe in spite of it, she couldn't stay away from him.

He drew her to him as surely as a compass is drawn to the north. She heartily wished there was some way she could maintain a level of casualness with him, but it seemed to be beyond her capabilities. She brooded over it for the remainder of the drive.

They passed through the town of Branaman and headed for the foothills of the Ochoa Mountains where they picked up a dirt road leading to the tallest peak, Branaman Mountain. They stopped so Dan could open the padlock on the chain-link gate, then drove through, leaving the gate open.

"Shouldn't we close that?" she asked, looking out the rear window.

Dan shook his head. "Someone from the Bureau of Land Management said for us to leave it open in case he needs to come through. I've got his only key. No one comes this way much, and they'll stay away altogether if they see this truck." He stepped on the gas and maneuvered around a bend in the dusty road.

Silvey held on for dear life as the four-wheel-drive truck bounced and roared up the rough track. Once, the back tires skidded sideways on the gravel and she grabbed for Dan's arm.

Grunting, he fought the wheel. "Silvey, if you cut off my circulation, I won't be able to drive."

"Oh, sorry," she gulped. She gripped the edge of the seat, preparing to scoot back and tighten her seat belt, but Dan slowed the truck and hauled her in close.

"Here," he said, lifting his shoulder and indicating she could tuck herself next to him.

Smiling shakily, remembering how it had felt to dance with him, kiss him, and forgetting all about casualness, she did so, pleased by his protectiveness.

Within a few minutes they stopped in a clearing just below a stand of pine trees. Dan switched off the motor and looked down at her. "Are you all right?"

"Yes." She eased away from him with an embarrassed smile. "I just didn't expect it to be this rough."

"Yeah, since the army dismantled their tracking station, this road hasn't been kept up. But we've arrived safely and we'll be finished in plenty of time before dark." He gave her a quick, all-encompassing glance to make sure she was all right and said, "Come on."

He jerked up the door handle and helped her out. They stretched and glanced around, then Dan led the way into the pines.

A feeling of reverence stole over Silvey, as if she was stepping into church. She looked sideways at Dan and saw the same feeling mirrored in his face, although his eyes were bright with eagerness.

At the edge of a natural clearing, he stopped and pointed. "Over there."

Her gaze darted ahead eagerly, then met his in disappointment. "That's it. Just dirt and rocks?"

He looked at her in amazement. "You were expecting marble headstones?"

"Well, no, but...." She didn't know what she had expected, but it wasn't this flat nothingness. "How do you know there's even anything here?"

As he started walking again, she hurried to catch up. "From the potsherds," he said, sweeping his hand toward the ground. "The places where they're the most dense is where the village was most likely situated." He pointed farther into the woods. "The largest concentration of potsherds was up there in another clearing. I'll take you up there in a minute. This burial ground was discovered by following a path that seemed to have been cut through the trees. One grave was excavated back in the fifties, before the missile tracking station went up."

"And before the laws prohibiting the opening of Native American graves," Silvey added dryly. "What was found?"

"Pots with supplies for the journey into eternity. One still contained a small amount of maize." As he spoke, Dan's voice grew in intensity and excitement. His face was eager.

Silvey smiled. She loved seeing him like this, open and free. "Tell me more," she invited, to keep him talking.

He swept her hand into his and led her around the edge of the burial ground, describing the way archaeologists created a grid of the excavation site, gave numbers to each section before beginning to dig carefully, sifting each spadeful of dirt to make sure nothing was missed. Each artifact was collected, classified, and carefully stored. Later it was placed in a museum for the public to view.

"Graves are an especially rich source of information," he went on. "Besides the pottery and jewelry that can be found, we can get a good idea of the state of health of the person. It's possible to find out what diseases, dietary deficiencies, wounds, they had. All this can lead us to know more about the tribe. What they ate, suffered from, what, or who they battled with."

Her forehead creased. "But you're an anthropologist."

His chin tucked against his chest as he drew back. "Well, what do you think archaeology is, if not the study of people? These subjects just happen to be long gone."

"But the sacredness of their burial ground... Would you like someone to go and dig up one of your ancestors?"

The avid gleam faded from his eyes to be replaced by a hint of exasperation. "No, of course not, but you have to admit there are no near relatives of these people to object."

"That doesn't make it right, Dan. Isn't there some way to study them without digging them up?"

"Sure, by using remote sensing equipment. It's a new type of technology, very delicate instruments that are passed over the ground to detect remains of manmade structures, telling exactly where to dig."

"So, why don't you use that?"

"Because little Sonora College can't afford it."

"Oh." She almost suggested that he could buy it himself. She knew he wouldn't because it would be too much like buying his way into the position of department head.

He pointed up the hill. "Come on. I'll show you the village site."

CHAPTER EIGHT

Silvey followed, her brown eyes studying his back, aware that he didn't know what more to say to her. He led her farther into the pines. The shade and coolness of the air were a relief after the midday heat.

Dan stopped at another clearing. "Here it is." He pointed toward a sunny area that was clear of trees. There were a number of dirt and rock mounds and she drew closer to examine them. A sense of wonder and excitement rushed through her as she imagined what the village must have been like at one time. Children would have been playing outside, the women working over their fires or tending their corn fields. The men would have been hunting or fishing, bringing home the day's catch to feed their families.

"My theory is that they used the rocks as part of their walls, mortared together with adobe."

"Weren't they farmers?" Silvey asked softly, her gaze drifting dreamily around the clearing. "My grandfather heard a little about it from his great-uncle, but even he couldn't remember much of what his ancestors had told him," she said regretfully. She wished she had paid more attention to the stories, knew some information that would impress Dan. She had made such an issue of protecting the Morenos' heritage, her heritage, yet she actually knew very little about them.

"Yes. They were farmers. They irrigated their crops by digging holding ponds for rainwater, which then dripped down to their fields." Dan strode around with swift, gliding movements, his gaze darting everywhere at once. Silvey could feel his excitement and interest. He fairly itched to begin excavating.

"I wonder why they left?"

Dan shrugged. "Any number of reasons. Drought, epidemics—either human or plant. Remember the Spaniards brought in diseases to which these people had no immunity. The tribe painted their skins brown with berry juice to ward off evil, which is why the Spaniards called them the Morenos."

"Too bad the berry juice couldn't ward off the Spaniards," Silvey murmured.

"They probably would have died out anyway, Silvey, because they were such a small group." Dan frowned at the ground. "The cause of this village's extinction might have been conflict with another tribe or village. They packed up what they could carry and went to greener pastures. There's actually a legend that says the village broke up because of greed and selfishness over their hunting grounds."

Silvey sat down on a lightening-struck pine that had been splintered ten feet up the trunk. Part of it angled to the ground, forming a seat where she could perch. "Do you believe the legend?"

Dan pulled a clean handkerchief from one of his pockets and began polishing his glasses. Without their transparent protection, his eyes looked exposed and thoughtful. "Maybe. I'd like to find out if there's anything here to indicate that it's true."

"And you could find out by digging here?"

"Yeah." His voice was thick with longing.

"There could be a lot left here, couldn't there?" Her smile was eager. "There could be buried pots, cooking utensils, arrows and spearheads. All kinds of things. And maybe some of them might belong to an ancestor of mine."

"It's possible," Dan conceded, giving her a curious look.

Silvey drew her leg up and wrapped her arm around her knee. Dreamily, she stared into space. "Just think, there might be something of my six times great-grandmother right here beneath my feet."

"That's possible, too." He glanced around, then sighed in frustration. "I don't want to see this site annihilated."

"Annihilated?"

"Silvey, there are people who would bring in skip loaders and scoop up the ground, destroying any hope of a planned, complete excavation."

"Who would destroy it?"

His eyes rolled at her naiveté. "Silvey, they're called pot rustlers. Anything of value from a tribe this obscure, such as a pot in mint condition, could bring as much as twenty thousand dollars from a collector."

Her mouth dropped open. "You're kidding."

"I'm serious," he insisted, urgency growing in his voice. "Because the Morenos were such a small tribe, anything connected with them has more value because of its rarity. For that kind of money, lots of people are willing to take the risk. With the military gone from here, it won't be long before someone tries it—and probably succeeds.''

"That would be tragic. The story of these people would be lost forever.''

"That's what I've been trying to tell you.''

She gave him a disgruntled look. "Well, you also said I needed to see this for myself, and I have. Other people should know what's here—and yet, if tourists were allowed in here unsupervised, the site would soon be destroyed.''

"And all this history would be lost forever.''

He returned to her side and considered her. "You sound like you don't object to excavating the village.''

"It's different than the burial site.'' One shoulder came up in a negligent shrug. "Besides, we both know my objections, or the objections of Leila's Warriors, aren't going to do very much to stop the excavation.''

He gave her a serious look. "Probably not.''

With a nod, she said, "I think you're right. I think people should know about the Morenos.''

"You changed your mind pretty suddenly,'' Dan said, giving her a skeptical look.

"It's different being here . . . seeing this. It would be wonderful if this could be preserved the way it is, but that's probably not going to happen, is it?''

A sympathetic smile touched his lips. "No, Silvey, it's not.''

"Then it's better if a responsible group does the excavation.''

"Do you mean to say I've convinced you?''

"Yes, I think so.''

Silvey squeaked in surprise when he let out a whoop that startled birds from trees. He reached out to haul her off the tree stump and into his arms.

"Dan," she gasped. "What are you doing?"

"Celebrating," he said, swinging her around. "I think I've actually hooked you."

Silvey choked on a surprised laugh as he twirled her a couple of times and she collapsed into his arms. He gave her a hug and she laughed, startled by the change in him.

His look was full of warm delight as he gave her a quick kiss and set her away from him. "I'm starved," he said. "I'll go back and get the food you packed and we can eat under those trees, away from the site. We don't want to disturb anything." He turned and loped away.

Silvey steadied herself against the scarred trunk as a startling revelation burst over her.

He had hooked her all right. Dan Wisdom had hooked her into falling in love with him. Her eyes followed him as he hurried through the trees.

She loved him—everything about him, his black moods and his sunny ones; his quick mind and his unshakeable honesty.

She loved him, but she knew he would never love her. To him, love was power, or maybe he equated it with physical attraction. Either way, he wouldn't love her. He'd vowed to give no woman power over him.

Defeated and dismayed, Silvey slumped against the tree, her hands limp at her sides. What was she going to do? Her whole life she had planned to love someone as Leila had loved her husband, as her own parents loved each other. She'd never expected to love someone who wouldn't love her back—who was determined to stay uninvolved.

It took her a few minutes to collect herself, but slowly her resolve built. He mustn't know how she felt. He would either disdain her love, or turn away altogether. She couldn't accept either, so she must never tell him. She rubbed her hands over her face, trying to wipe away the distress. By the time Dan returned, she had dredged up a smile.

They spread their picnic under the trees, on a soft bed of pine needles that had probably lain undisturbed for decades. Silvey set out the packages of sandwiches and the neatly sliced vegetables. Dan opened the sodas and handed her one, then settled back against the trunk of the nearest tree. Their companionable silence was broken only by the call of birds and the occasional raucous squabbling of the squirrels. Once, she thought she heard the sound of a car motor, but it was cut off suddenly, leaving them in peace.

Silvey ate slowly, keeping her thoughts to herself as she tried to come to terms with what she had just discovered about herself. She stole sidelong glances at Dan, noting the easy way his back rested against the tree, the methodical way he demolished more than half the sandwiches. When he was finished, he sat with one knee raised, and his forearm resting on it.

She loved to look at him when he was like this, relaxed and without his usual wariness. Why couldn't she have fallen for a guy who was a little easier to understand, to get close to?

"Have I got mustard on my chin?" he asked suddenly, turning his head to look at her.

"What? Oh, no." Dismayed that she'd been caught staring, Silvey quickly gathered up the leftovers from their lunch, stuffed everything back into the hamper, and mumbled, "I'll take this back to the truck." She hurried down the hillside to where the truck stood, put the hamper in the back, then walked back to where Dan was still lazing under the tree.

All the while, she reminded herself to play it cool. If she wasn't careful, she was going to give her true feelings away.

She returned to the village site and began moving carefully around the clearing, her footfalls muffled by the padding of needles underneath. When she heard the sound of a branch snapping, she turned in that direction, thinking she might see a deer, but all was still. She moved back to the lightening-struck tree.

"What was unusual about the Morenos, Dan, that they kept themselves separate from the other local tribes?"

"They were metal workers for one thing. They had developed methods of smelting small amounts of copper that no one else knew. It's been said they wanted to keep the secret to themselves. They made jewelry from it and traded with other people from as far away as the coast of Baja, California." He stood and ambled over to her.

Silvey leaned against the trunk. "Just think, there were whole systems of government, trade, cultural values in place all over this continent that were destroyed forever by the coming of Europeans."

"Exactly." Dan gave her a penetrating look, then glanced around.

Thoughtfully, Silvey stood and placed a foot on the tip of the pine, then brought her other one up behind. What Dan had said earlier was horrifying. There was a rich culture here to be explored and it would be a crime for thieves to get here first. If only it didn't include digging up graves. She sighed as she moved lightly up the trunk.

"You'd better be careful. You might fall."

She glanced down in amazement. "Dan, have you forgotten what I used to do for a living?" She turned, bent over backward until her hands were against the rough bark, and did a walkover, flipping her feet easily so they landed near her hands. If the trunk had been smoother, she could have done the splits. Coming upright on the narrow log, she lifted her hands and bowed to her audience of one.

Grinning, Dan shook his head and applauded.

Silvey ran down the trunk, Dan held up his hand in invitation and she took it to jump down beside him. A pebble flew up and wedged beneath the tongue of her boot. With a sound of disgust, she bent to dig it out. It was dark green and as she started to toss it away, she heard a dull metallic thunk.

Glancing down sharply, she examined it. "Dan, look! It's shaped like a bell. With a tiny clapper and everything."

Dan's breath hissed in. "Let me see." Reverently, he held out his hand and she dropped it into his palm. He turned it, examining it minutely while she all but danced with impatience at his side.

"Well? Well?" she prompted, crowding him, getting in his way, blocking his light.

He looked at her, excitement shining in his eyes. "It is. Silvey, it's a copper bell. God, what a find."

"Really?" She fell to her knees and began feeling gingerly through the leaves and pine needles. "Maybe there's more."

"If there is, we shouldn't...."

"Wait." With a shriek of delight, Silvey loosened the dirt around a hard object, then pulled it free of the dirt. It was another tiny bell, but this one was attached to a whole string of them. "Dan, look. I think it's a necklace."

Dan came down beside her and took it from her hands into his own. He stared at it in awe and Silvey gave a tiny laugh. "Dan, your hands are shaking."

He swallowed, closed his eyes, then opened them and looked at her. "Silvey, this is the most significant thing you could have found—that anyone could have found. It gives a whole new dimension to the people here, gives them real personality and depth. Look at this." He held it out. "See how the bells are shaped?"

Silvey examined them. They were straight-sided rather than made in the traditional flared shape to which she was accustomed.

"The Morenos dedicated certain shapes for specific ceremonial objects."

"Oh?" Silvey looked up, her eyes shining. "And what was this for?"

"It's a bride's wedding necklace, passed from mother to daughter."

Silvey's face went blank. "You're kidding."

"No. I've only seen one other, in a museum in New Mexico."

"Dan," she breathed reverently, taking the necklace into her own hands, "one of my ancestors might have worn this."

"It's possible."

In awe, her fingers trembling, Silvey lifted the necklace to her own throat. She gazed down at it. Encrusted with dirt, the green-tarnished bells lay against her yellow shirt. She didn't see the grime, though. Instead, they were perfect—brightly polished red-gold in color. She imagined generation after generation of Moreno women wearing this necklace, their numbers stretching back into time.

She might be a modern woman whose Moreno blood had been diluted by decades of intermarriage with other races, other cultures, but she felt a connection to these women of the past.

Her eyes were full of tears and her lips were trembling when she raised her head to meet Dan's eyes.

"I didn't know," she said, her voice cracking. "I honestly didn't know."

Dan reached out to tuck a strand of hair behind her ear. His fingers stayed to caress her cheek. "Know what?" he asked softly.

"How...how it would feel to find something like this."

"It's a kick, isn't it?"

"Yes." She placed her hand over her pounding heart and, with an embarrassed laugh, blinked away the tears. At last, she drew in a shaky breath. "This is wonderful."

"It's priceless."

Gingerly, she dusted some of the dirt from it and started to slip it into the pocket of her shorts.

He caught her wrist and smiled in sympathy even as his eyes seared into hers. "You can't do that, Silvey. This isn't an official site. We have permission to be here, but not to dig here."

She gaped in disbelief, her brown eyes wide. "But what if someone comes along and . . . ?" She broke off, horrified.

"At last, the light dawns," Dan teased. "This is what I've been trying to tell you. Pot thieves have no right to it, but they could easily take it."

Silvey straightened her spine and her lips drew together. "We'll see about that." Turning, she stepped onto the trunk of the pine and lightly ran up to where the tree was split. As Dan watched, she dropped it into a small depression in the hollowed trunk thrusting from the ground and nodded smugly. "There. No one will find it now."

When she came down, he was watching with an admiring gaze. Before she reached the last few feet, he lifted his arms, clasped her around the waist and set her on the ground before him. "You may be a little too clever. I don't know that I can walk up there and retrieve it," he said, jerking his chin toward the stump.

She tossed her head, her golden-brown hair swishing against his hands across her back. She cast him an upward glance through her thick lashes. "Then you'll just have to bring me up here again."

Excitement steamed through her veins at the sudden heat in his eyes. His cleanly honed features, dappled by the shadow of a nearby aspen, were intense as he stared down at her. "You know, I'm going to have to do something about your tendency to flirt."

Her heart started to flutter like a wild bird caught against a window screen. "Oh? Like what?"

"Maybe I'll have to make sure you flirt only with me."

Smiling seductively, she placed her hands on his arms. "I think that can be arranged—but you have to catch me first." She shoved downward, freeing herself, and turned to dash away. Although his legs were longer, she was smaller, and fast, and she had the element of surprise on her side.

He didn't call out for her to come back or stop, but she could hear his boots pounding the ground behind her. She didn't dare look to see how close he was, but dashed wildly back the way they had come skirting the burial ground and heading for the truck. She planned to get inside and lock the doors, teasing him. A few stones rolled beneath her feet, throwing her off balance, but she righted herself and kept running.

Her mad race was made even more exciting by a sudden wind that had kicked up, sighing through the pines and tossing the shivery silver leaves of the quaking aspens. She dashed through the wind, feeling it whip her hair and pull at her clothes. She looked back once to see Dan several yards behind. He was running as hard as she was, legs and arms pumping, his face set. Laughing, she put on another burst of speed.

Exhilarated, her legs stretched to their fullest length, but she could hear Dan gaining on her.

She broke from the woods and spied the truck. Convinced she could make it, she kept running. Within inches of the vehicle, she felt something brush her shoulder, then return to grasp it.

"Gotcha," Dan growled, spinning her around and falling with her against the door.

Gasping, her head dropped back. Her eyes were full of laughter. Dan's were keen, his gaze touching on her flushed features and landing on her half open, panting lips. He leaned toward her, one hand on each side of her.

Silvey's eyes drifted shut, knowing he was going to kiss her, wild with anticipation and the memory of the last time he had done so.

Dan touched his lips to hers, softly and gently. They were both still winded from their sprint. His breath puffed out, mingling with hers, adding power to his touch and taste.

"Silvey, I knew the minute I saw you that you would lead me a merry chase."

"I'm so glad I've lived up to your expectations."

Dan reached up and pushed tendrils of hair from her face. Silvey went still at his touch, her concern growing at the troubled look coming into his eyes. "Maybe my expectations of you have been too harsh."

Silvey reached up and touched his cheek. "What do you mean?"

He surprised her by turning his head and placing a kiss on her fingertips. "Never mind. We'd better get in the truck and..." He stepped back and looked down, frowning.

Disappointed that he didn't finish what he'd started to say, Silvey sighed and followed his gaze downward.

"What the...?" he muttered.

She turned with him and they saw that the vehicle was sitting at an odd angle. Both tires on the right side were completely flat.

A sharp, succinct curse split the air as Dan hunkered down beside the truck and examined the tires. "I can't see anything, but whatever it was got both tires. I must have hit a piece of metal, or something." He stood up and gave the vehicle a disgusted look. "But I didn't notice anything wrong when I came back for the basket."

He turned, his narrowed eyes searching her face. It took Silvey a full minute to realize what he must be thinking. She drew herself up, her eyes snapping. "The truck was perfectly fine when I brought the picnic basket back, Dan. There was nothing wrong with the tires."

The wind picked up, tossing Silvey's hair into her eyes and mouth. She swept it back and anchored it behind her right ear as she gave him a defiant look.

Dan studied her face for a moment, noting the tilt of her chin and the firm line of her mouth. "Don't get your nose out of joint. I believe you."

She blinked at him and gave a firm nod. "Well. Good. That's good. So what are we going to do?"

Dan gestured with his chin. "We'll have to walk into Branaman and get a tow truck—if one can be found on a Saturday afternoon in a sleepy desert town."

Dismayed, Silvey glanced down at her boots. Her feet were hot and uncomfortable. "Walk? How far?"

His gaze followed hers. "About five miles. Sorry, but I'm afraid there's no choice." He lifted his head and studied the sky. "I think we're going to have to wait a while, though."

She looked up to see that he was examining the sky above the desert. From their vantage point on the bare slope of the mountain, they could see an enormous brown wall moving toward them. "Oh, no." Her shoulders rounded in defeat. "A dust storm."

He squinted against the lowering sun. "Yeah, and headed this way. We'll have to wait in the truck until it blows over."

"Good idea," she agreed, reaching for the door handle. "I don't want to drive through that."

They climbed in and poured themselves refreshing drinks of water from the bottles Silvey had brought, sharing a cup, then settled back to wait out the storm.

She turned sideways on the seat, facing Dan. He had one arm across the back of the seat and the other on the rim of the door. One long leg was crooked at the knee so that it curled around the gearshift.

"I don't suppose you've got a deck of cards on you?" she asked, glancing at the multiplicity of pockets on his clothes. "We could play gin."

He cocked an eyebrow. "You play?"

"Are you kidding? What else is there to do when you're stuck in a backwater town in Georgia or Mississippi, the last performance is over and the streets have been rolled up and put away for the night?"

He tipped his head back and laughed, then looked at her with speculation gleaming in his eyes.

"You know, we have some unfinished business that could keep us occupied."

"Oh?"

He leaned forward, watching her face. "Yeah. I caught you, we're here alone together, and now you have to learn your lesson about flirting."

The confines of the truck cab were suddenly stifling. Silvey watched the purpose in his eyes and blurted the first thing that came to mind. "Have you got anything to eat?"

"Eat? You just had lunch."

"Well, you ate most of the sandwiches."

He sat back, his expression telling her he knew exactly what she was doing and he was going to let her get away with it—for now. "Yeah. I've got some beef jerky."

He pulled a canvas bag from under the seat and unsnapped it to draw out several strips of the dried meat and a pocket knife. He handed both to her.

Silvey took them reluctantly. She didn't want to appear ungrateful, but she didn't care for beef jerky. To her, it tasted like old dried bologna.

"You asked for it," Dan commented, correctly reading the hesitation in her movements.

"This will be fine, thanks."

"Just cut off a chunk the size you want," he said.

Silvey glanced up suspiciously, sure she heard suppressed laughter in his voice. Her chin jutted out stubbornly as she took a piece of the dried meat in one hand and pried the blade out of the knife with the thumbnail of the other hand. When it came free, she stared at the encrusted metal in repugnance. "What have you been doing with this knife?"

"Performing autopsies."

Horrified, she looked up. "Yech!"

On a burst of laughter, he took the knife from her, scrubbed the blade with a clean bandanna and some water from a bottle, carved off a chunk of the meat and handed it over. "Just taste this. I think you'll like it."

Hesitantly, she bit down on the tough meat, then looked up in surprise. "It's good."

"When are you going to learn to trust me?" he murmured, watching the pleasure in her face. "I make it myself. Fresh meat, herbs and spices. I dry it in my barbecue."

"Ah, a man of ingenuity who's handy in the kitchen," she said, settling back against the door and chewing happily. "What more could a woman want?"

Dan laughed again and cut off a chunk for himself, then twisted around to watch the approaching dust. "You'd better eat fast if you don't want a mouthful of dirt. Here it comes."

She did so and washed down the chewy meat with another gulp of water before the already-listing truck was rocked by gusts of wind. Her hands shot out, one to the dash, the other to the seat back. "Do you think this is safe?" she shouted over the roar of the wind and the sound of dirt pelting them. Within seconds, a fine fog of dust filled the cab.

"We don't have any choice," Dan said. "We can't get out in this. Here." He lifted his hips from the seat and pulled the large bandanna out of his back pocket once again. He handed it to her. "Hold this over your nose."

"But then you won't have one!"

He threw his hands skyward. "I wish, just once, you could do something without arguing. Come here." He reached over and hauled her up between his knees, turned her and settled her on the seat. Her bottom was nestled against him and his arms secure around her. He pushed his chin down onto her shoulder, shook out the handkerchief, and spread it over both their faces. "Hold it over your nose," he growled in her ear.

Too stunned to do otherwise, she obeyed, taking a corner of the fine blue-and-white cloth and covering her nose. Breathing was instantly easier, if she didn't count the way her chest was constricted by having him practically surrounding her. She shivered.

"It's going to be all right, Silvey," he whispered in her ear, tightening his arm around her waist. "I won't let anything happen to you."

She believed him and closed her eyes against a sudden rush of tears. She was in love with him, probably since that first night he had appeared out of nowhere to protect her from an imagined fear.

Surreptitiously, she tried to blot her tears on the bandanna, but they were too close for him to miss what she was doing. While the wind rocked them, dirt pelted them, and dust tried to choke them, he put his lips to the base of her neck and kissed her. He didn't push it any farther because he was offering comfort, but Silvey felt as if she had been given a gift of infinite value. She relaxed and tried to empty her mind of her doubts and fears, reveling in the feeling of safety he gave her.

The storm continued for almost thirty minutes, until Silvey was sure the poor truck had been scrubbed bare of every last speck of paint. In spite of the bandanna, she had enough dust in her eyes, nose and throat to choke a buffalo. At last the wind began to lessen, then died down to a soft breeze. Dan scooted her forward on the seat and she turned to look at him. Simultaneously, they burst out laughing.

"You look like the Abominable Dust Man," she gasped.

"You don't look much better."

Besides what they had breathed in and swallowed, they were covered with a fine sifting of sand. It coated their hair, eyebrows, eyelashes, skin and clothes. The only clean place on each of them was the circle around their noses and mouths. Gamely, they climbed out of the truck to shake some of the dust off.

Silvey pulled her hairbrush out of her bag and tried to get some of the dirt out of her hair, but finally gave up. She tossed the brush back into her bag and said, "We might as well start walking."

Dan looked down at her feet. "Are you sure you want to?"

"You're not leaving me alone up here!"

"Okay, you asked for it." He took her hand and they started off down the rutted track.

By the time they reached the dirt road into Branaman, the perspiration had turned the dust into mud. It was caked in the creases of their skin and they teased each other as they trudged along.

This had to be love, Silvey decided as her skin began to itch and her feet grew more and more uncomfortable in the sturdy hiking boots. She wouldn't be enjoying this annoyance with anyone she wasn't nuts about.

After a few minutes on the road, a vanful of fisherman picked them up, gave them a ride into Branaman, and dropped them at a service station that had a tow truck.

While Dan and a station employee went after the truck, Silvey shut herself in the small restroom and attempted repairs to her hair and makeup. She only succeeded in filling the little room with a fog of dust and the small sink with mud.

Gazing at herself in the mirror, she grimaced and muttered, "I look like I've been mudwrestling. How can Dan resist falling madly in love with someone who looks like this?" With a shrug, she gave up and stepped outside.

In a little while, Dan returned with the tow truck and the driver set about changing and repairing the tires. Dan cleaned up and they went to a nearby fast-food restaurant to get something to drink. When they came back, the station owner met them, shaking his head in puzzlement.

"I don't understand it. There wasn't a thing wrong with those tires. Just needed air."

Dan pulled out his wallet to pay the man. "I'll talk to the school's vehicle maintenance office. Maybe the tires are faulty."

Silvey couldn't mourn the problem. In spite of the inconvenience, she didn't regret the day.

It was growing dark by the time they climbed into the truck and headed back to Tucson. She started to take her place by the door, but Dan reached over and drew her to him, tucking her

behind his shoulder and smiling down at her.
Sighing happily, she fastened the center seat belt,
and laid her head on his shoulder. No, she didn't
regret the day at all.

CHAPTER NINE

WITHIN two hours they were back in Tucson and it had grown dark. As promised, Dan stopped and bought her a car battery. She tried to protest when he paid for it himself, but when he gave her a level look, she subsided. She smiled to herself when she thought about their first meeting, their dispute over money, something that didn't seem to matter to him at all now. Next, he took her to the convenience store near her home and installed the battery in her car. Once the car was running, he followed her home and walked her to her front door, unlocked it, and flipped on the lights.

She did as she was told when he ordered her to stay put while he performed a quick security check of her home. Never mind that she had traveled all around the nation in a circus caravan and spent many nights in places far less safe than this. He was being thoughtful, and really, she didn't mind being cherished. In fact, it was something she could become accustomed to in a very short time.

Dan returned to her, and standing by the entrance, he pulled her against him, wrapping his arms around her waist. She placed her forearms along his biceps and her hands on his shoulders.

He brushed her lank, dusty hair back from her face and looked into her eyes solemnly. "I want you to think about all you saw and all we talked about today, Silvey."

"I will."

"Silvey, I know you've changed your mind about the village site, but you've got to think about the burial site, too. I don't want to fight you on this issue," he said, his voice dead-level serious, "but I will if I have to. It's important that it be examined scientifically and saved from thieves or vandals."

Silvey's brown eyes were shadowed by worry. "And this excavation has nothing to do with your possible promotion?"

"No, of course not."

She gazed at him for a moment. She knew he was honest, sometimes too honest. "I believe you," she finally said.

"And then you make a decision about whether or not to oppose me and what I'm trying to do."

Her dirt-streaked face turned up to him. "I will," she repeated.

One corner of his mouth edged up. "You're so agreeable tonight. I'd better take advantage of it." He lowered his head and his lips covered hers.

She responded instantly, her feelings for him surging to the surface, swamping her with need. She curled her fingers into his khaki shirt, smelling the dust, tasting his unique salty sweetness. His muscles flexed beneath her fingers as if he was tensing, preparing himself either to pull away or to pull her closer.

After long moments of shared delight, he eased himself back, his breathing as ragged as hers. "This is getting to be a habit, Silvey."

Her gaze flew up to see the seriousness in his eyes. "If so, it's a very nice habit."

He smiled slowly. "I can't argue with that."

"In fact, you could almost say it's getting very close to involvement."

His eyes darkened. She thought they almost looked sad. He didn't answer, but instead, he turned, using one of those incredible, controlled movements of his. He spoke over his shoulder. "Better get some rest. Good night." He ducked out the door and disappeared down the walk.

Silvey refused to allow his mood change to affect hers. She knew there was a battle going on inside him. All she could do was hope that the two of them were on the same side, and that they would win. Together.

She shut the door behind him and leaned against it for a moment, her fingers pressed to her lips. Smiling dreamily, she floated across the living room, headed for the shower. The ringing phone intruded into her happy thoughts and she detoured to pick it up.

"Hello?"

"Hello, Silvey, is that you?" Reed Madison's voice boomed over the line.

She grinned. "Yes, Reed, it's me. Who else would it be?"

"Where have you been girl? We've been trying to call you all afternoon. You'll never guess what we did."

A shiver of apprehension skipped up her spine. She squelched her first reaction, which was to groan in frustration. "Remember, Reed, you weren't going to do anything without discussing it with me first?"

He cackled in triumph. "This was a chance too good to miss."

"Oh, Reed, I don't think I like the sound of this."

"You'll like it, trust me."

Silvey pulled the receiver away and gave it a skeptical look. He was the last person in the world she would trust to use good judgment. With a sigh, she said, "Okay, what did you do?"

He paused, obviously savoring his big moment. "The Beltrans and I took a little drive out to Branaman Mountain this afternoon. We saw a Sonora College truck up there and let the air out of the tires!"

Silvey made a strangled sound. "Oh, Reed, you're joking."

"Nope. That'll teach 'em a thing or two about who they're dealing with."

"Yes, Reed," she snapped. "It certainly will." She hung up quickly before she could give the old man a piece of her mind.

She would have to call Dan right away, and apologize. She reached for the phone again, then decided this might be better faced in person. After all, she was responsible for the group, even if she had ended up being their victim.

She was going to call her grandmother and tell her she wanted no more to do with Leila's Warriors. They were a group of loose cannons racketing around on the deck of their own little ship, crashing into things and causing endless trouble.

She headed for the door, but checked herself, remembering that she was still filthy. Fuming, she stomped into the bedroom and grabbed clean underthings, then dashed into the bathroom.

Silvey showered quickly, combed her hair and left it to air dry, and pulled on a kelly green sundress and matching sandals. She dabbed on a minimum of makeup, grabbed her purse, and headed out the door. It took her a few moments to recall the address she had memorized along with Dan's phone number when she'd sneaked a peek at his checkbook. Finally, she headed east, into the foothills of the Santa Catalina Mountains.

She took a few wrong turns, but finally located Dan's house on a quiet street of impressive new homes with security fences and yards carefully landscaped with desert plants.

Silvey parked in his driveway. When she stepped out of her car, motion-sensitive lights flooded the front of the house with brightness. Blinking, she made her way to the front door and rang the bell. When there was no answer after several tries, she walked around to the side where she found an unlocked gate.

Curious about the sound of splashing water, she pushed her way through, and found herself in an enclosed patio, surrounded by tropical plants. She was looking down at an illuminated swimming pool whose luscious waters lapped at the tile.

It took Silvey only a few seconds to realize that the splashing sound she had heard was made by Dan, who was methodically swimming laps.

"Amazing," she muttered. "We hiked all over a mountain, walked a couple of miles to reach the road, and he comes home and swims laps. This guy could be the poster person for self-discipline."

In spite of her grousing, she couldn't help admiring the way he sliced through the water in clean, even strokes. His powerful arms seemed to carry him in bursts with carefully timed help from kicks of his feet. When he reached the end of the pool, he somersaulted under water and started the return lap.

Silvey decided it would probably be a while before he was done, so she looked around for a chair. Might as well be comfortable while she waited. Besides, she wouldn't mind sitting and watching him for a while. She found a lounge chair in a darkened corner of the patio and perched on its edge to enjoy the show.

He swam ten more complete laps before he stopped and rested, drawing in deep breaths. Then, he placed his hands on the edge of the pool and in a surge of power, sprang out of the water and onto the pebbled cement.

That was the moment that Silvey realized that a man swimming alone in his own backyard didn't necessarily bother with a swimsuit.

Her gasp of surprise had his head whipping up. In what seemed like one movement, he grabbed a towel, wrapped it around himself, and leaped across the space dividing them.

Within seconds, Silvey found herself flat on her back on the lounge chair with Dan holding her down, his forearm across her throat.

"All right," he growled. "Who are you and what are you doing here?"

"Dan." she choked. "It's me. Silvey."

He straightened in surprise and loosened his hold on her neck. "Silvey? What the devil are you doing here?"

"Learning how to breathe through my ears," she gasped.

"Sorry about that." He helped her sit up, then turned so that he was sitting beside her. He rubbed her back solicitiously until she could catch her breath.

"I... tri-tried your doorbell but there was no answer so I came around back. The gate was unlocked so I came on in."

"Why didn't you let me know you were here?"

"You were busy," she said with a quick, sideways glance, sharply aware of his warm, moist thigh pressed against hers. "I didn't want to interrupt you."

"So you decided to give me a little added cardiovascular workout by presenting me with the shock of my life when I finished."

Silvey lifted her chin and met his eyes in the dim light. "You came out of that pool buck naked. *I'm* the one who got a shock."

He grinned. "Excuse me for not taking into account that there might be a peeping Thomasina in the neighborhood."

"I forgive you."

"My fault," he said. "After that trip up the mountain, I should have invited you to come swimming with me."

She looked at him from the corner of her eye.

He laughed. "I would have worn a swimsuit."

"It's probably just as well. As dirty as we were, we would have clogged up your pool filter."

Dan stood and pulled her to her feet. "Come on in and you can tell me why you came over." He stopped and swung around suddenly, anxiety shadowing his eyes. "It isn't Dad, is it? Or Leila? Did you hear something from them? Because if you did..."

"No," she reassured him quickly. "Nothing like that, but I do have something to tell you."

He ushered her through wide arcadia doors to a family room with burgundy carpeting and cream-colored leather sofas. The walls were covered with floor-to-ceiling bookcases, each one filled with volumes. The room opened onto an eat-in kitchen with a butcher block work island in the center, wide counters topped with Mexican tile, and the very latest in modern kitchen equipment—a homemaker's dream.

Dan disappeared down a hallway and Silvey took the opportunity to examine his books. She had seen his office and the artifacts that were displayed there. She was surprised to see that in his home, there were few such artifacts. Most of the books were novels and well-worn reference volumes on pre-Colombian history. On a modest shelf, she found copies of his own mystery novels, as if they'd been placed there as an afterthought. A computer and printer covered the top of an oak desk. Yellow legal pads, scribbled with notes were stacked beside it.

This was where his alter ego, D.K. Wilinson, did his writing. Silvey was tempted to sneak a look at his latest project, but she resisted the urge. She knew that was something that he definitely wouldn't like.

She longed to explore the rest of the house, but she knew she wouldn't get the chance. As soon as she told him what Reed had done, he would probably escort her out and never speak to her again.

Dan was back within a few minutes, dressed in a loose white T-shirt and cutoff jeans that gave Silvey a new appreciation for a man's legs. Funny, she'd never realized that bare feet could be sexy. His hair, which he'd finger-combed, was mussed and inviting.

Silvey sighed inwardly. She really had it bad if she was getting dreamy over Dan's feet and messy hair.

"So, what's this important news that couldn't be relayed over the phone?" he asked. "Not that I mind your unexpected visit."

He swung the refrigerator open, grabbed a couple of cans of soda and popped them open as he came toward her.

He invited her to sit on the sofa opposite him and she did so, teetering nervously on the edge.

"I guess I could have called, but...I thought you might hang up on me and this is the kind of thing I need to say in person."

Dan's eyes grew serious. "So say it."

"The tires on the school truck aren't faulty. They were deflated deliberately by some of Leila's Warriors."

He set his soda can down on the table in front of him. "Excuse me?"

"Some of the people from the group were up on the mountain. They must have seen the open gate, followed us in, saw the truck and...." Silvey shrugged. "Come to think of it, I thought I heard a car. It might have been them. I guess the opportunity was too good for them to miss."

"The opportunity to cause me trouble was too good to miss, you mean."

Silvey's brown eyes were full of misery. "I'm sure they didn't know it was you. They just saw a chance to cause mischief and took it."

"And these are adults we're talking about here, right?"

"In a manner of speaking."

Dan stared at her for a second before he spoke. The careful tone of his voice told her he was very angry. "I thought the idea of us going up there together was that you'd see the true picture and call them off. You didn't have them follow us, did you?"

Irritation replaced the misery in her eyes. "Oh, certainly. I just love being caught in a sand storm, then having to walk a couple of miles to get help in changing flat tires."

She jumped to her feet and started for the door, but Dan was right behind her. His hand on her shoulder was light, but firm. "Silvey, sit down."

She jerked away from him. "I don't want...."

"I said, sit down." He urged her back to her seat. "I want to get to the bottom of this."

Slowly, to show him that she was doing this only because she chose to, Silvey returned to her place on the sofa. He sat down beside her, but she pointedly drew her skirt away. He frowned at her, but she tossed her hair back and lifted her chin.

With an irritated sigh, he stood, towering over her. "The business with the tires was just a prank?"

"That's right."

"And you knew nothing about it?"

"Right again."

"In that case, I believe you."

Expecting more of an argument, Silvey was surprised by his quick affirmation. A smile tickled at her lips as she stared at him. "You do?"

"Yes, but they're going to have to stop doing this kind of thing."

"Yes, I know, but Grandma's the only one who can control them. They rarely listen to me."

"So why did you agree to watch out for them?" He held up his hand. "Never mind. I know the answer to that. It's that loyalty thing I've noticed about you."

"What?"

"I think we've discussed it before."

"You think I'm too loyal to my grandmother?"

"No, but you let your loyalty blind you to good judgment."

She crossed her arms and gave him a sardonic look. "Oh, really? This little insight into my character is just too fascinating. Please go on."

"You take up with old friends you haven't seen in years as if they two of you are caught in some kind of time warp and neither of you has changed."

"Now you're talking about John Ramos, aren't you? I haven't 'taken up' with him," she responded tartly.

"Only because I've been around to stop you."

Silvey didn't even bother disagreeing with him. He obviously had something on his mind and she wanted to know what it was. If he would ever get to the real point of this discussion.

"Dan," she said, helplessly, "I don't know what you're leading to."

He turned and paced the room. "Silvey, I've told you that I don't know much about women like you...and your grandmother. Honest women. Dad seems to attract women of somewhat inferior character,'' he added dryly.

Silvey remembered every word he'd said. "Yes. Your stepmothers were mostly opportunists as I recall.''

"Bloodsuckers,'' he snorted.

"Not all women are like that.''

"I know. I guess the images I formed in childhood loom larger than they should.''

"We all have things we carry around with us.''

"That's true.''

She thought about that for a few seconds. "Dan, surely not all the women you've been with over the years have been like that.''

"No, they haven't. I deliberately chose women who were independent, successful in their own right.''

"Ones who knew the score,'' she added.

His smile was quick. "Right. They didn't ask more than I was willing to give and I didn't ask more than they were willing to give.''

Silvey wrinkled her nose. "Sounds boring.''

"Maybe, but the truth is, some of my images of women are...horrifying.'' He paused, obviously deciding whether or not he should continue. "When I was sixteen, one of my stepmothers offered to teach me a few things about love.''

Appalled, Silvey stared at him. "That's disgusting.''

"That's what my dad said when he kicked her out that very day and started divorce proceedings.''

"Good for Lawrence,'' Silvey said fervently.

Dan came over and sat down beside her. Picking up her hand, he curled his fingers around it. "I work with good women. As I said, I've dated women who were honest about what they wanted out of a relationship and so was I."

"Bully for the both of you."

Oblivious to her snippy comment, Dan went on. "I thought that would be the best way to avoid Dad's mistakes, but it's made me cynical."

It had been the best way he had known to protect himself, Silvey thought, with a flash of insight. Even a strong man had his vulnerabilities.

"I judge too quickly and too harshly, I know that I do. It's not something I take pride in," he finished.

In his own backhanded way, Dan was apologizing. Silvey curled her fingers around his. "But you recognize it and you try to make it right. That's why I love you."

Dan had been looking down at their linked hands. Now he went very still, then turned his head to stare at her.

"Repeat that, please," he demanded in a hoarse voice.

Silvey opened and closed her mouth a couple of times, then gave a helpless little moan. "I can't believe I said that. It fell right out of my mouth. I didn't even know it was coming."

"But you did say it. Now repeat it."

Silvey swallowed, though her throat was as dry as the Sonora Desert. "I . . . I said I love you."

"Damn, Silvey," he murmured, closing his lips over hers. He slipped his hands up her arms, his fingers dipping beneath the shoulder strap of her dress to massage, and then lay bare the delicate bones there. His lips followed his fingers to caress her collar bone. His hands moved down to encircle her waist, then moved up to rest just short of her breasts.

The shock of it had her gasping, but she didn't want him to stop. When his lips returned to hers, she responded eagerly. He had kissed her before, but it hadn't been like this. He had kissed many women before, but she hoped it hadn't been like this. His other kisses had been appreciative, full of desire, but this was intense. This was from his soul.

Responding to him, she felt her heart pound, her skin heat. Her hands flew to his shoulders, his neck, his hair, filling themselves with the damp thickness there. Somehow that made him more real—more earthy.

When he pulled away, his eyes had deepened to midnight. "Silvey," he said in a raw voice. "I can't tell you I love you. I haven't seen enough real love to know what it looks like."

She laid her hand on his cheek. "Oh, Dan, it's not something you see. It's something you feel."

He pressed his forehead to hers. "Honey, what I'm feeling right now has more to do with lust than love."

"Lust, hmm? That's a start." Her teasing smile flickered and died and the last words she would have expected from herself tumbled from her lips. "Let me stay tonight, Dan."

He shut his eyes and a shiver ran through him. "Silvey, no."

Rejection hurt. Pulling her pride around her like a protective cloak, she tried to sit up. "Oh, well, if that's the way you want it...."

He held her in place. "It's not the way I want it. But it's the way it's going to be. You're not the kind of woman for a quick affair, or even a long term one."

He'd said that before, but pride be damned. She wasn't giving up without a fight. "You mean, I don't 'know the score'?"

"Honey, you don't even know what inning it is."

She had to smile at that because it was so true. He was so far outside her usual experience that she didn't even know what step to take next. She had known him for less than three weeks and her mind had scrambled almost every minute to keep up with what her body wanted.

"Come on," he said, standing and helping her to her feet, "I'll walk you to your car."

She knew this was for the best, but Silvey still stung from the rejection. Or at least she did until they reached her car and Dan pulled her close. He rested his hands at the back of her waist and swung her gently from side to side.

"What say we forget this whole business of elderly rabble-rousers, Moreno burial grounds, my father, your grandmother, and every other damned thing that's been between us since the minute we met and get down to some serious dating?"

"Dating?"

"You know. The old-fashioned kind of stuff where we go out and listen to concerts that bore us to tears, see movies we hate, and explore overpriced restaurants."

She laughed and went on tiptoe to kiss him. "Sounds great. When do we start?"

"Tomorrow. I'll pick you up at seven. I seem to remember that you're a hell of a dancer."

"So are you."

"Then we'll go dancing."

"I can't wait."

Silvey slipped into her car. Dan slammed the door, with a reminder to fasten her seat belt.

She was tempted to remind him that it was a state law to do so, but she kept quiet. He might be overbearing, but she was beginning to realize that some of the things he did were to show he cared.

She figured it was about the next best thing to love.

Silvey backed out of the driveway and drove away, grinning at stop signs and streetlights, thinking this business of falling in love wasn't so bad after all. A girl just had to be careful that when she fell, she landed with the right man.

CHAPTER TEN

DURING the next few days, Silvey and Dan were together whenever they weren't working. He complained that his new mystery novel wasn't getting written and his deadline was fast approaching. She answered back that she barely spent any time in her new shop, but she knew that neither of them would have changed things. Her only disappointment was that he wasn't in love with her yet, but she had hopes.

She had carried through with her threat and called Leila to resign her position as unofficial overseer of Leila's Warriors. Her grandmother had accepted her decision and apologized for expecting it of her. Silvey assumed Leila had called the members of her group and had a stern talk with them because she heard no more from them. It was with a sense of relief that she turned her attention to her time with Dan and to her new business.

Whenever she talked to Leila, though, she was reminded that Dan hadn't yet become reconciled to his father's forthcoming marriage. Silvey never missed an opportunity to praise her grandmother, but Dan usually met these statements with a knowing grin. Eventually, Silvey began to realize that no matter what she said about Leila, the change to a permanent commitment had to occur in Lawrence—and in Dan. As much as she wanted to fix things for Leila and Lawrence with Dan, she knew it had to happen naturally.

One afternoon Dan dropped by the shop and waited with barely controlled impatience while she prepared strawberry sundaes for a couple of little girls. When her customers were seated with their treats, he commandeered her attention by planting his hands on the polished glass countertop, leaning over it, and giving her a kiss.

"I got clearance to begin excavating the village site on Branaman Mountain."

A month ago it would have infuriated her. Now Silvey was thrilled for him. She reached across the counter and gave his hand a squeeze. "Oh, Dan, that's great. Congratulations."

He smiled, then gave her a searching look. "Are you okay with this?"

"Yes. I feel differently about it than I do the burial site. And, well, I realize now that you're good at your job."

Ignoring the giggles from her two little customers, he kissed her again. "I guess I'll have to keep trying to change your mind about that burial site. Gotta go. We start tomorrow and I've got to get my equipment ready."

"Tomorrow? I didn't know you could start so soon."

"No reason not to."

"No, I guess not," she said, swallowing the disappointment in her voice. It had just occurred to her that between the two-hour drives back and forth to the mountain, and his book deadline, she would hardly ever see him.

He seemed oblivious to her concern, and she wasn't going to spoil his happiness by telling him what she was thinking.

She dredged up a smile and waved as he swung through the door and headed for his car. With a resigned sigh, she returned to work.

The next evening, Silvey was at home, sitting in her favorite chair with her bare feet tucked under her when someone rang the doorbell. The nightly news was on, but she was watching with little interest, so she didn't mind the interruption. Hoping it was Dan, she jumped up, smoothed her hair, and hurried to the door.

A man she had never seen before stood on the porch. He was short and stocky, with iron gray hair and the bearing of an ex-military officer. Before she could offer a greeting, he said, "Are you Silvanna Carlton?"

"Why, yes." She glanced past him to see a car with the Sonora College logo printed on the side. "What can I do for you?"

"Miss Carlton, I'm Bob Fillmore, head of security at Sonora. I was wondering if you would be willing to accompany me to the college." As he spoke, he flipped open his wallet and showed her his identification.

Silvey barely glanced at it before giving him a puzzled look. "Accompany...?" Fear clutched at her heart and she swung the door wide. "Dan. Has something happened to Dan... Dr. Wisdom?"

Her visitor shook his head in a quick, sharp negative. "Not in the sense you think. But there is something that he and Dr. Varga would like to discuss with you."

"Dan sent you? Why didn't he come himself?"

"Perhaps you can ask him that when we reach Dr. Varga's office."

Silvey stared at him for a few seconds. This man was giving nothing away. She supposed it would be okay to go with him, if Dan needed her, but why hadn't Dan called?

Silvey glanced down at her clothes. Her cotton leggings and loose T-shirt weren't something she would normally wear to go out, but she didn't think Mr. Fillmore would be willing to wait while she changed.

"All right," she said uncertainly. "I'll get my purse and my, uh...shoes."

Mr. Fillmore waited while she gathered her things and locked the house. He held the car door for her with utmost courtesy, but said hardly anything on the drive to the college. Even Silvey's usually outgoing nature was quelled by his reserve.

The college looked deserted when they arrived. Mr. Fillmore parked in an empty slot by the administration building and held the door for her while she stepped from the car. He was close by her side as they walked into the building. Silvey gave him a nervous look, wondering why he was hovering so. She had the crazy urge to see what he would do if she suddenly made a break for it.

He took her to Dr. Varga's office, where they found the college president sitting behind a massive desk. Dan sat in a chair nearby. Both men seemed to be waiting in grim-faced silence, but they stood when she entered.

In spite of Dan's unwelcoming expression, Silvey walked straight to him with a smile. "Hello, Dan. How did your excavation go today?"

To her surprise, she thought she saw pain flash through his eyes, but he merely nodded toward a chair and said, "Why don't you sit down, Silvey?"

More alarmed than she'd ever been in her life, Silvey backed up until she felt the chair seat against her legs, and sat down shakily. "What . . . what is it, Dan? Dr. Varga?" She glanced around and saw that Mr. Fillmore had taken a chair opposite her so that the three of them were lined up on one side of the room with her alone on the other.

Dan started to speak, but Mr. Fillmore held up his hand. "Maybe I'd better start, Dr. Wisdom."

Dan answered with a sketchy nod, never taking his eyes from Silvey's face.

Dr. Varga tented his hands on top of his desk and sat forward, looking at her over the tops of his bifocals. "Miss Carlton, we decided to begin this matter here and see if we can get to the bottom of it before we call in the police."

"What matter?" she asked, her gaze darting from one to the other of them, then she caught the last part of his statement and gasped, "Police?"

"It's about the necklace, Silvey," Dan added. Despite his agreement to let Dr. Varga question her, Silvey could see that he wanted to be in control.

"What necklace?" she asked. "Why don't you three stop with the terse questions and come right out with it?"

"All right. We were trying to spare you, give you a chance to explain," Dan said. "We want to know what you did with the Moreno necklace that you found at the Branaman Mountain site.''

"What *I* did with it? I walked up the trunk of that tree and put it in the top of the stump, remember? You stood right there and watched me.'' She gave a small laugh as relief flooded her. "Is that what this is all about? Did you forget which tree it was?''

"No, I didn't forget which tree it was," Dan answered, his brows drawn together in a fierce frown. "I did watch you put it in, but what we want to know is when did you go back and take it out?''

"When did I . . . ? What are you talking about?''

"The necklace is missing. When did you take it out?''

"I *didn't* take it out. Why would I?''

"Any number of reasons," Mr. Fillmore broke in authoritatively. "Maybe you wanted to make a point. Dr. Wisdom tells us you've been opposed to the excavation.''

"You think I *stole* it?" Disbelief and horror washed over Silvey and her eyes shot to Dan's face. When she had first walked in, she had thought he looked grim. Now she realized he was cold and distant. His eyes were examining her in the impersonal way he might look at a potsherd or a specimen—not as if she was the woman who loved him.

She shook her head slowly from side to side. "Dan, you don't believe that, do you?''

The expression in his ice blue eyes didn't alter by so much as a degree. "I can only believe the evidence of my own eyes. I saw you put that necklace into the tree after I told you we couldn't remove it from the site.'' His lips drew together in a thin, straight line. ''You tried it on. I saw the look on your face....''

''But...but that doesn't mean I....''

''When I got permission to do the excavation and returned to the site today, the necklace wasn't there. You and I were the only ones who knew where it was and I know I didn't take it.''

Silvey put a hand to her throat where her pulse pounded against her palm. ''And so that automatically makes me the guilty person, right?''

Dan gazed at her for a few seconds. Finally, she saw emotion begin to move in his eyes, but the emotion she saw didn't comfort her. It was pure rage. His voice was flat when he answered her. ''I don't see any other explanation.''

Hurt sliced through her heart so sharply, it was physically painful. Dazed, Silvey looked down to see if she was bleeding.

''Do you have another explanation, Miss Carlton?'' Dr. Varga asked.

''How...how could I? I don't know anything about this. I didn't take the necklace.''

''Come, come, Miss Carlton.'' This time it was Mr. Fillmore speaking in an impatient, no-nonsense voice. ''It was there when you and Dr. Wisdom left the site and it isn't there now.''

''I don't know where it is. I didn't go back and take it. How could I? There was a lock on the gate and I certainly don't have the key.''

''But you're an acrobat,'' Dan said quietly.

She turned to him, tried to focus on him, but it was as if she was caught in a nightmare where things shifted and changed, and made no sense. "What?"

"You could have climbed the fence with no problem. You showed me how easy those kinds of stunts are for you, remember?"

She remembered. She remembered everything about that wonderful day. She remembered how she'd realized that she was in love with him. Didn't that mean anything? She looked at his face.

Obviously not. He didn't believe her. He really didn't believe her.

Mr. Fillmore moved in his chair as if anxious to be done with this. "Miss Carlton, we're questioning you here because we understand you have a personal relationship with Dr. Wisdom."

Silvey's face burned, but she spoke defiantly. "Not anymore, I don't," she said.

Dan sat forward, then stood and moved to stand before her. "Just tell us what you did with it, Silvey, and we'll get it back and forget this whole thing."

Love meant nothing to him. Nothing. She had been building air castles when she thought he could love her. He had told her he hadn't seen enough love to recognize it. He hadn't felt enough to know what it felt like, either.

In a sudden, blinding spurt, her hurt was replaced by pure, savage fury. She shot to her feet and stood with her hands clamped onto her hips.

"You can just forget this whole thing right now," she insisted. "I'm sorry that necklace has disappeared, but I didn't take it. What would I want with it?"

"You speculated that it might have belonged to one of your ancestors."

She stuck her chin out. "That's not proof that I took it!"

"The necklace is of great historical value, which means that to somebody it had great monetary value."

"Then hadn't you better be looking for someone who needs money?"

"You needed money," he observed pointedly.

Hurt surfaced again, but she fought it down. "And I made the mistake of accepting a loan from you. That's going to change," she said recklessly. "You'll get your money back faster than you can shout 'stop thief,' and...."

"I don't want the damned money back," he said through his teeth.

"No." She pointed a finger at him and made jabbing motions a few inches from his chest. "You want me to give you back a necklace that I don't have, didn't take, and don't know where to locate."

"You and I were the only ones who knew where it was," he said, reaching out and grabbing her hand, firmly but inexorably in his own. "We were the only ones on that mountain."

"Are you sure? Remember the flat tires?"

His eyes sharpened. "Do you think those crazy old people took...?"

"Oh, of course not. The way they bumble around, we would have seen them. And if they'd tried to climb over the gate after we locked it they would have broken their necks."

Dan went very still, staring at her as if an idea was forming in his mind. His hand went lax so Silvey was able to pull hers away.

Seeing the newly intent expression on his face made her think he was about to come up with some fresh accusation against her. Crippling sorrow warred with hurt and anger inside her. She had to get out of that office or she was going to be sick.

She took a deep breath, forcing it past the lump of misery in her throat. "I'm leaving, gentlemen," she said, her furious gaze sweeping the room and coming back to Dan's stony face. "Since I didn't take the necklace, I suggest you concentrate on finding the person who did."

Head high, she stalked from the room. She heard Dan say something short and urgent to Mr. Fillmore as she hurried down the hall.

She was only a few steps from the building's front door when Dan caught up with her. His hand wrapped around her upper arm and brought her around to face him.

"Wait a minute, Silvey."

"No," she said. To her horror, tears started into her eyes. She turned her face away so he wouldn't see them. "I'm leaving."

"You don't have your car. Come on. I'll drive you home."

Open-mouthed, she stared at him. "What in the world makes you think I would accept a ride from you?"

"You have no choice." Maintaining his grip on her arm, he started off. "You'll either ride with me, or I'll carry you home. Either way, I'm taking you there."

Silvey wanted to dig her heels into the carpet, but she knew he would simply pick her up and carry her. With a hop and a skip, she caught up with him, jerked her arm from his grasp, and stomped along beside him, down the hall and outside to his car.

He unlocked the door and waited until she was seated and had her seat belt fastened before he closed the door. He obviously thought she would jump from the car and run away if he didn't watch her every move. She should do it, she thought in disgust. It would confirm everything he already thought about her. She wouldn't give him that satisfaction, though. She was completely innocent.

In unrelenting silence, she folded her arms across her chest and sat that way through the entire ride to her house.

When they pulled into her driveway, she had her seat belt off and the door open before the car stopped rolling. "Don't bother to see me inside, Dan. This is the last we'll be seeing of each other."

"That's what you think," he growled, following her from the car. "I'm coming inside."

Silvey was on her porch by this time, her key poised for the lock. She turned to him and laughed in disbelief. "Absolutely not. You've done enough harm to me today. Go away."

"No." He took the key from her hand and unlocked the door, then stood by resolutely as she flounced inside.

In her living room, she slapped the light switches on and cranked the air conditioner up to full blast, even though she doubted it would do much to cool her anger. Finally, she turned on him.

"Don't you know when you're not wanted, Dan? Go away."

His jaw clenched as he stared at her. "I'm waiting for something."

"For me to throw you out? Or for me to call the police?"

His sharply defined features grew harsh. "You can't do the first, and you won't do the last."

"Just watch me." She started for the phone.

"Silvey," he said calmly. "I'll just tell them my fiancée is upset and having prewedding jitters."

Her hand on the phone, she swung around to gape at him. "Your...?"

"Fiancée," he supplied.

Inarticulate with rage, it took her a few moments to form a reply. "Well, when she shows up—whoever the poor, unlucky girl is—maybe she can help me throw you out."

Dan walked to her and removed her hand from the telephone. "You won't want to do that—and stay off the phone. I'm expecting a call."

Silvey made a strangled sound and whirled away from him. She picked up the first thing she saw, which luckily for him, turned out to be a small pillow, and hurled it at his head.

He caught it easily in one hand and tossed it onto the sofa. "Why don't you go make us something to eat, Silvey? It'll help the wait go faster."

"If you think I'm going to feed you, you really are crazy!" But it was an excuse to get away from him while he waited by the phone, though, so she whipped around and strode from the room.

In the kitchen, she jerked the refrigerator door open and removed items for sandwiches, which she carried to the table. Seating herself on one of the chairs, she began slapping together sandwich after sandwich until she had used an entire loaf of bread, then she sat staring at the mound of sandwiches and wondered if she was losing her mind.

The wild maelstrom of emotions she had experienced in the past two hours began to calm and focus on the thing that hurt her the most.

She was in love with Dan Wisdom, but he distrusted her, thought her a thief. She had been a fool to think he would change, would come to love her. She offered him her most precious gift, her love and trust, and he'd thrown it right back at her.

Silvey pushed the sandwiches away, laid her head on the tabletop, and began to cry in great, gasping sobs that came up from the depths of her soul.

She didn't know how long she sat like that, trying to purge her being of the sorrow, and of the love, but the next thing she knew, she felt Dan's hand on her head.

She turned her head to dislodge it, but he said, "Silvey, listen to me."

"I've listened," she mumbled. "I don't want to hear any more from you." She lifted her head and stared at him with red-rimmed eyes full of accusation. "I loved you, but that didn't matter to you."

"It mattered," he answered grimly.

"Oh, yes, sure it did. It mattered so much that I was the first person you thought of when that necklace turned up missing." She stood up to face him and threw her hands wide. "Of course. I'm the obvious suspect. I'm a woman, aren't I? I'm a woman who needed your money, therefore I'm willing and able to do whatever is necessary to keep taking things from you, I...."

"Shut up, Silvey, before you say something you'll regret."

"The only thing I regret is falling in love with you, but, fortunately, that's not a permanent condition. It can be cured like appendicitis, or...or...."

"It was John Ramos."

The statement was so unexpected, she stopped and stared. "What?"

"Bob Fillmore just called. The thief was John Ramos. He's got the necklace and was trying to find a private collector to buy it."

Silvey leaned weakly against the table. "How...did Mr. Fillmore find out?"

"You told me, and I told him to question Ramos."

"How could I have told you? Are you saying you think I knew that...."

"No, no." Dan held up his hand, then he ran it over his face. For the first time, Silvey could see that he looked haggard and exhausted. She refused to believe it had anything to do with her and fought down the surge of compassion that filled her heart.

"I'm explaining this badly," he said.

"You do seem to be better at accusations than you are at explanations."

Dan gave her a steady look and she subsided. "When we were in Dr. Varga's office, you said we needed to be looking for someone who needed money. Then I remembered that you're not the only acrobat I know."

"John," she said softly.

"Yes. He qualifies on all counts. He's always poor-mouthing about the money he has to pay to his ex-wives."

"Did he follow us, and . . . ?"

"Yes. After he dropped you off at your house that morning, he followed us up to the mountain and onto the site—remember I had to leave the gate unlocked—and saw us find the necklace. He's a dishonest idiot, but he's no fool. He knew how valuable it was. He probably figured it would be weeks before I got permission to excavate and when the necklace was discovered missing, I would suspect some anonymous pot rustler."

"Instead, you suspected me."

Dan's face spasmed. "I'm sorry, Silvey. I didn't know what else to think."

"You could have trusted me."

"Trust and love go together, Silvey, and we've already established that I don't know much about love."

"You don't know anything about it," she sighed, beginning to turn away.

"I'm learning, Silvey. I'm learning fast. I know I love you."

Her head came slowly around to face him. "What did you say?"

"I love you, Silvey."

Hope fluttered in her chest, but she ruthlessly shoved it down. "You can't. You don't know anything about it."

"I know I was a damned fool to think you had anything to do with a theft. I know you're not like any other woman I've ever known." He took a step toward her. "I know I wouldn't blame you if you told me to get out of your life, but I hope you won't.''

Silvey shook her head and covered her face with her hands for a moment. ''You can't change this quickly. Two hours ago you thought I'd committed a crime, now you're saying you love me.''

''I've been in love with you for a long time,'' Dan said, moving close, reaching up to pull her arms down. ''I just didn't recognize it for what it was.''

Silvey let her hands drop. ''I . . . I guess you can't recognize something you've never seen before.''

''I guess not.'' Dan pulled her into his arms and rubbed his cheek against hers. His eyes were squeezed shut as if he was trying to block out pain. ''Tell me I haven't blown this completely. Tell me that you still love me.''

''Yes.'' Happiness flooded through her when she admitted it. ''Of course I do. Love doesn't die because one partner does something stupid.''

''Keep telling me that,'' he advised, bending his head to touch his lips to hers. ''Whenever I do something stupid, keep telling me that.''

Love for him poured out of her and into the kiss she gave him. She wrapped her arms around his neck and clung to him, all the pent-up love in her generous soul pouring out to envelope him. ''I love you, Dan.''

He kissed her again, then drew away. ''I meant what I said. If you'd called the police I would have told them you were my fiancée. I'd already decided to marry you even when I was mad as hell at you.''

She gave him a knowing look. "Which probably made you think you were exactly like Lawrence, which probably made you even madder."

His grin was sheepish. "Yeah. I had it all wrong about him and Leila. I should have realized that even though his other marriages have failed, at least he's had the courage to keep trying."

"And you didn't even have the courage to try it once."

He grimaced. "You know me so well."

"Good," she said, settling into his arms. "Let's keep it that way." She leaned back and looked at him again. "Does this mean you're not going to object when Leila and Lawrence are married?"

"No, I won't object. In fact, I think we ought to make it a double wedding."

"Really?" She stood on her toes and threw her arms around his neck. "I'd love that."

They were quiet for a few minutes, each lost in their own thoughts. Finally, Dan nudged her away from him and looked into her eyes. "So I take it that's a yes? You'll marry me?"

Silvey gave him a solemn look. "I will as long as you remember that I'm a once in a lifetime kind of wife."

"Honey, you've got yourself a deal."

The double wedding took place in October at the village site on Branaman Mountain which had dressed itself in red and orange for the occasion. Leila wore a long, tailored dress of pale yellow, and Silvey wore a traditional white gown.

The idea of having the weddings on the mountain had been Dan's. Silvey had been enthusiastic, especially after he had given her a Moreno wedding necklace that he'd had handmade for her by a local jewelry craftsman.

Leila had been against the idea until Lawrence had declared that he'd had five weddings in churches or chapels and none of them had lasted— maybe getting married outdoors would change his luck. Leila had dryly pointed out that this marriage would last because of the person he was marrying, not because of luck, but she'd agreed to the outdoor setting and had enthusiastically entered into the preparations.

Silvey took a deep breath of the spicy fall air and watched as yellow aspen leaves gave up their grip on twigs and branches and drifted to earth on the slight breeze. Some of them landed on the roped-off village site, which was yielding more and more information about the Morenos as the excavation continued. After Dan had been named department head, he had purchased the remote sensing equipment that located promising areas for excavation.

As for the burial site, Dan had decided to excavate the graves, document the contents, then cover everything up again. When all the documentation was finished, the state park service had agreed to take over the site, thus helping to protect it from pot rustlers. Silvey was happy with the plan, considering it to be the best compromise.

More aspen leaves fell, landing on wedding guests, who stood waiting for the ceremony to begin. They cheerfully brushed them aside as they chatted and listened to the violin and cello music which was being provided by a group of Sonora College students.

Silvey couldn't imagine a more perfect setting for her wedding, here in the place where her ancestors may have lived.

As the musical piece ended and the students prepared to begin "The Wedding March," Silvey's father, Richard, took her arm. Leila clung to his other arm, speechless with excitement.

Silvey looked up at him and grinned. "Are you ready to give away both your mother and your daughter?"

"No," he said bluntly. "But I'll do it, anyway."

Silvey laughed and hugged his arm, then glanced over and winked at her mother who smiled back. "I'm so glad you and Mom could come."

Richard glanced ahead to where Dan and Lawrence had taken their places beside the minister. "You're our only daughter," he tilted his head. "And she's my only mother. I had to be here for this—and I had to check out the men you two are marrying." He hesitated, meeting her eyes. "You're sure you know what you're doing?"

Beneath a stand of pines, Dan and Lawrence waited. They were dressed in dark suits, but sunlight speared through the branches, burnishing them in autumn's golden light.

Dan met her eyes and smiled. Silvey was thrilled to see that there were no shadows there. He was as sure as she was.

Happily, Silvey looked up at her father. "I know exactly what I'm doing, Dad. And I'm glad to be doing it."

He laughed, then firmly clasped both her and Leila in a hug. When the first notes of the march sounded, the three of them joined arms and stepped out together.

New York Times Bestselling Authors

JENNIFER BLAKE
JANET DAILEY
ELIZABETH GAGE

Three *New York Times* bestselling authors bring you three
very sensuous, contemporary love stories—all centered
around one magical night!

It is a warm, spring night and masquerading as legendary
lovers, the elite of New Orleans society have come to
celebrate the twenty-fifth anniversary of the Duchaise
masquerade ball. But amidst the beauty, music and revelry,
some of the world's most legendary lovers are in trouble....

Come midnight at this year's Duchaise ball, passion and
scandal will be...

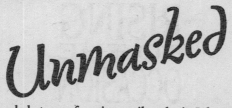

Unmasked

Revealed at your favorite retail outlet in July 1997.

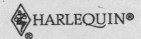

HE SAID

♥

SHE SAID

Explore the mystery of male/female communication in this extraordinary new book from two of your favorite Harlequin authors.

Jasmine Cresswell and Margaret St. George bring you the exciting story of two romantic adversaries—each from their own point of view!

DEV'S STORY. CATHY'S STORY.
As he sees it. As she sees it.
Both sides of the story!

The heat is definitely on, and these two can't stay out of the kitchen!

Don't miss HE SAID, SHE SAID.
Available in July wherever Harlequin books are sold.

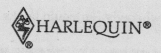

HARLEQUIN®

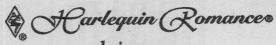
brings you

SIMPLY THE BEST

Authors you'll treasure,
books you'll want to keep!

Harlequin Romance just keeps getting better and
better...and we're delighted to welcome you to our
Simply the Best showcase for 1997, highlighting a
special author each month!

These are stories we know you'll love reading—again
and again! Because they are, quite simply, the best...

Don't miss these unforgettable romances coming to you
in May, June and July.

May—GEORGIA AND THE TYCOON (#3455)
by Margaret Way
June—WITH HIS RING (#3459)
by Jessica Steele
July—BREAKFAST IN BED (#3465)
by Ruth Jean Dale

Available wherever Harlequin books are sold.